D0991325

AFTER
THE WEDDING

Hila Colman **AFTER THE WEDDING**

William Morrow and Company
New York   1975

Copyright © 1975 by Hila Colman
All rights reserved. No part of this book may be reproduced
or utilized in any form or by any means, electronic or mechanical, including photocopying, recording or by any information
storage and retrieval system, without permission in writing from
the Publisher. Inquiries should be addressed to William Morrow
and Company, Inc., 105 Madison Ave., New York, N.Y. 10016.
Printed in the United States of America.
1 2 3 4 5   79 78 77 76 75

Library of Congress Cataloging in Publication Data

Colman, Hila.
  After the wedding.

  SUMMARY: A young couple discover after they are married
that their philosophies of life are not as compatible as they
had imagined.
  [1. Marriage—Fiction. 2. Divorce—Fiction]
I. Title.
PZ7.C7Af   [Fic]   75-11587
ISBN 0-688-22043-6
ISBN 0-688-32043-0 lib. bdg.

AFTER
THE WEDDING

I

"Getting married's a big thing," Peter said. "It's the biggest thing I ever did in my whole life." We were sitting in a dark booth in Pat's corner store on the West Side of New York City, but I could see Peter's blue eyes looking at me solemnly through his glasses.

"We don't have to," I told him. "Just as long as we're together." Not together in the mechanical way some of our friends were—one couldn't go for a walk without the other—but independently together, doing what each needed or wanted to do and still sharing our lives. Peter and I had talked about it a lot. We thought and felt the same way about not pushing or wheedling the other. We couldn't stand those endless discussions about what movie should we see, or where should we eat, or what should we eat. If one of us wanted to see a movie and the other didn't, one went and the other did whatever he felt like doing. That was the way we wanted to live.

"No. No way. I want the real thing," Peter said. "I'm getting used to the idea of getting married. I like it."

I was glad. It was his way of saying all the things that I felt. I mean, falling in love was one thing, but loving someone like Peter, who was so absolutely in tune with me, was another. A girl can fall for a fool too and have a disaster. I couldn't believe my luck.

When I left Peter that afternoon it was after seven o'clock but still light. I walked down Eighth Avenue thinking, in four days we're going to be married . . . ninety-six hours. And then I went into a panic. What if he got hit by a truck, what if someone knifed him? I ran down the crowded street, knocking into kids, saying excuse me to old ladies with shopping bags, as if getting home meant safety. But there was no safety except where Peter was and where we would be together, away from the confusion of living in separate houses, the hassle of the city, the interference of school and jobs, of involvement with things and people we no longer cared about.

At Twenty-second Street I ran toward Seventh Avenue. I ran all the way until I came to our house. Dirty words written all over the walls, people getting mugged in the hallways, in the tiny self-service elevator. But the apartment was rent-controlled— that was the big thing in our family. A tenant couldn't complain to the landlord about the peeling paint, the roaches in the kitchen, the muggings, the lack of heat or hot water. If he didn't like it, he could move and make the landlord happy. The landlord could get double and more from a new tenant.

The apartment itself wasn't bad. It was on the sixth floor and had lots of space. That and the low rent kept us there: my mother and father, my kid brother, and me. Except I was getting out. I was marrying Peter. The words were a song in my head, with beautiful music. I really loved that guy, not that I thought he was perfect. He could be pig-headed and stubborn—Mom said all men were. But knowing Peter's faults didn't bother me; they were just a nuisance once in a while.

Down the hall in the living room I could hear my father declaiming about the wonders of some obnoxious shaving cream he would use only if he got paid, and we all had our fingers crossed that he would. He was rehearsing for a TV commercial audition the next morning: "I used to hate shaving . . . a man with a tough beard like mine sometimes has to shave twice a day, but when my wife gave me. . . ." Poor Dad. I adored him, but he was one of the reasons that Peter and I were planning our lives differently.

Dad was convinced he was a great actor, and maybe he was, but few people seemed to agree with him, and his life was one disappointment after another. There were times when he'd had some pretty good runs in soap operas—we had steaks in the house then—but sooner or later he'd be written out of a show and we'd go back to hamburgers. Mom's salary as a teacher would be our only income, and Dad would go into a deep fit of depression. He'd never played Hamlet or King Lear, and we all knew he never would.

But Peter and I agreed that our lives were not going to be dependent on professional careers. We had no ambition to make money or to be commercial successes or to own things. No ranch house and Ethan Allen furniture for us. We resented even buying new jeans and only did when the old ones fell apart.

When I first met Peter, he was already thinking this way although he had come to New York with other ideas. He was going to a radio and television school, learning to direct and produce as well as the technical stuff, and also working as a page boy at NBC where Dad met him. A tall, sturdy, serious boy who'd come to New York from Mason City, Iowa, to make it big.

Dad brought him home for dinner one night— one of the steak nights—and he talked show biz to this kid, Peter Lundgren, a mile a minute. Mom and I were serving dinner when all of a sudden Dad said, "My daughter Katherine was named after Katherine Cornell, one of the great ones."

Poor Peter nodded and smiled and said, "Yes, of course," but I knew instantly that he hadn't the vaguest idea who Katherine Cornell was. He was not to be believed. He'd been up in the Empire State Building, had walked across the Brooklyn Bridge, and memorized where all the subways and buses went.

"You make us born and bred New Yorkers feel ashamed," Mom said.

"It would probably be the same if you came to Mason City, Mrs. Holbrook." Peter was terribly polite.

When my brother Larry—named after Sir Laurence Olivier, who else?—came in, late as usual, Peter got into a conversation with him, and I decided Peter was a stuckup creep and went to my room. Who was he to pay no attention to a girl who played the Fairy Queen in sixth grade and once was voted the girl with the best laugh of anyone in the class? Besides men whistled at me, and even Larry admitted my figure was good and my hands strong for a girl. As I brushed my hair furiously, I figured that Peter probably liked girls with tons of make-up, the kind you see walking on Madison Avenue carrying Gucci handbags and hat-boxes, who think they're actresses or models, and end up demonstrating lipsticks at Bloomingdale's, if they're lucky.

I didn't care. I was going to live my life differently. Then I did what I always do when I'm disturbed. I took a hunk of clay and started making something. I didn't know what it was going to be when I started, but working clay with my hands does something beautiful for me. My room was filled with objects I had made: bowls, mugs, pitchers, weird animals, a small Indian lady with a round, fat baby on her back. The only problem was that a lot of them would dry up and crumble because they hadn't been fired. Only the things I had made in the class at the Settlement House, where I had first learned about pottery, had gone through the kiln. But someday I was going to live in the country where the air was sweet, in a little house where I could see trees and grass, and where I'd have a kiln. I was only eighteen, but I was angry. Angry at the way life treated people in the city, at the shoving and the noise and the dirt, at the need to be rich to have anything beautiful. In the country a person could at least see the landscape, even if he didn't own it.

The second time Peter came to our house it was in the afternoon, and I stayed in my room. I wasn't going to go out to greet him because he was tall and well built. Probably he thought he was God's gift to women.

My door was open and when my father went out to get cigarettes, Peter walked in. "You make all these?" he asked, indicating my pottery. A dumb question, because he could see I was working on a bowl. I had rolled the clay out with a rolling pin and kept it on a form overnight. Now I was building it up, piece by piece.

I nodded my head. "Yeah."

"Don't they need a glaze or something?" He was examining some pieces close up.

"They need to be fired." I went on with what I was doing.

"Why don't you do it?"

I raised my eyes to look at him. "Because it's too much of a hassle to carry pottery around New

York." One dumb question after another. "The kitchen oven's not hot enough." I thought I'd tell him before he asked.

"You mean you just go on making these, and they'll never be finished so they can be used? It seems kind of a waste." His eyes and his tone said, "You must be a nut."

"I like to do it," I said tersely, hoping I got across the point that it was none of his business.

"You must," he said amiably. "You should have a kiln. You could buy an electric one."

I put down the bowl I was shaping and pushed back the long hair falling over my face. "I intend to have a real outdoor one someday." Then I saw something in his face and a gentleness in his hands as he picked up one of my pieces admiringly that made me blurt out more than I had intended. "I'm going to have a place in the country and a kiln and do nothing else all day but make pottery. I'll do it too," I said defiantly, as if he had argued with me.

"Terrific," Peter said, and sat down at the end of my worktable. "That's what I want to do—live in the country. When I first came to New York, I thought it was great. But I've had it. I made a mistake, and I'm not ashamed to admit it. I'm going to finish school and get out. Find a job in some small radio station out in the sticks." His grin was candid and adorable. "I'd rather be a big shot in a small place than nothing here."

"Do you have to be a big shot?"

His face became serious. "No—only for myself in a way. Not in the make-a-lot-of-money sense, but I have to do something that I believe in, to satisfy me."

Maybe that was when I fell in love with him. I don't know. Afterward Peter kept coming around but not to see my father. We were both busy, he at school and his job and I working in a flower and plant shop in the Village, so we met at odd hours and never had enough time. We'd sit in a coffee shop and talk and talk, and then we'd have to leave in the middle of a sentence to get where we had to go. Before long we knew that we both wanted to be together in the same place.

One day my mother said to me, "You sure you know what you're doing, wanting to isolate yourself in the woods someplace? You're a city girl, and I think you have a romantic notion about what living in real country is like. You'll get bored."

"I don't think so. It's not just a simple matter of the city or the country. It's a whole different way of life. You and Dad love the city, but Peter and I are in different places."

"What do you mean *different places*?"

"We don't like to put people down if we think differently, so we say we're in different places. Peter and I are in the same place."

"I hope so," Mom said, not sounding very convinced.

When we were lucky enough to have days off at the same time, Peter and I would go to the bus terminal or the train station and get on anything that was going to the country. We'd travel to some town that sounded interesting, up in Connecticut or New York State or even as far as Massachusetts. We'd get off at the town and walk and walk for miles even if the weather was bad.

In the spring we got serious about finding a place to live and getting married. Peter would finish school in June. We both became terribly excited when we made the decision, at Nathan's on Eighth Street of all places, and rushed home to tell my parents. Mom got teary, and Dad ran out to get a bottle of champagne. Peter called up his mother in Iowa—his father had been dead for several years —and introduced me to her on the phone. I felt like an idiot, because I didn't know what to say, and she just kept asking, "Where did you meet? Where did you meet?" She said that Peter must finish school and that it had been raining all week. I

18

couldn't believe I was talking to my future mother-in-law, and privately I was relieved that she lived way off in Mason City. I had never thought about Peter with a family, because he seemed to be part of ours, as if he'd been dropped on our doorstep out of the sky, or I should say out of the big NBC studios. Sometimes I thought of him as having been a waif living in one of their corridors, except that he was so big and independent he didn't fit the image.

And now in four days we were going to be married, and I still had to sew my wedding dress. No lace or satin and chiffon for me. My mother wanted to buy me a dress, but I had told her that I'd rather make what I wanted.

Mom had been looking anxious for weeks. "You're both so young," she said to me one day. "I worry about you. Two idealists. . . ." She shook her head. "At least with your dad and me, I have a steady job. I'm the practical one."

She wasn't telling me anything I didn't know, but she was putting herself down. "You're pretty idealistic, too. You've believed in him all these years, haven't you?"

My dear mother blushed. "I love him," she said simply.

"And I love Peter. Don't worry, Mom, you'll get

wrinkles. We'll be okay. I'm strong and tough, like you," I added with a grin.

My mother laughed. "I wish the kids in school thought so. They've got me down as a softie."

I knew what she meant because I wished I was as strong and tough as I sounded. As Peter had said, getting married was a big thing. The thought of being someone's *wife* sounded awesome and a real responsibility. You can love someone and be certain that you want to get away from home and start a new life and still be scared of your own decision.

I was working on this big no-iron sheet, turning it into a monk's robe with a hood—I knew exactly how I wanted to look—when Larry came into my room. "You going to wear that thing?" For a four-teen-year-old he could get a real contemptuous look on his face.

"Yes, I'm going to wear it."

"You're a kook."

"Get out of here," I yelled at him. Damn! I didn't want to be one of those dumb, nervous, tense brides that you see on Saturday night TV shows.

I printed a big sign that said *Enjoy* and hung it over my sewing machine.

2

Our wedding was sweet and funny, sort of like an old Charlie Chaplin movie. We kept moving around and talking like people in a silent film with the voices and music dubbed in, forming tableaux and speaking in a slightly formal, artificially polite way. "Would you care to sit down?" "May I pour you another glass of wine?"

Mom's living room was the right setting: old-fashioned and solid, shabby genteel. Dad's friend, the judge who married us, was the most elegant person there. He drank too much, kept saying he had to kiss the bride, and pinched my bottom so often that Peter stopped thinking it was funny. Peter's mother, a sweet, gentle lady, couldn't quite believe we were married because the ceremony didn't take place in a church. She was too polite to say so, but she did ask to see our marriage certificate and looked it over several times with her reading glasses on. The only other people there, besides my family, were Sam Levine, a friend of Peter's from school, and Judy Kuwolski, my oldest friend whom I had known since third grade.

"I pronounce you man and wife." We really kissed, not one of those dumb pecks, and I thought for a minute I was going to swoon from the excitement of it.

We spent our wedding night and the next few days in Peter's crummy apartment. I mean really crummy, although I discovered that Peter was terribly neat. He's a very organized person; in the morning he made lists of things he had to do, and he did them. He said that with his schedule he couldn't have survived otherwise. It was sweet to see him write down, "Take desk to Sam's apt., Get Katherine's clothes, Pick up check at NBC, Buy shoelaces." I wrote at the bottom of one of his lists, "Love Katherine," and he said he didn't need to be reminded.

I couldn't believe we were really together. That I could wake up in the middle of the night and he'd be there, curled up next to me, and still be there in the morning so we could have breakfast together. Peter adored cheese, and we'd have great breakfasts of dark bread and hunks of cheese, and sometimes we ate crazy things like chili and beans, because we could do anything we wanted to do.

We were terribly busy preparing to move upstate to a funny, little house we had rented. We had found it on one of our trips to nowhere, and this house was truly out in nowhere. We had gone to Lake Copake, which had sounded pleasant, and discovered that the place was dotted with ugly cottages. But we fell in love with the surrounding countryside and went back. Splurging, we rented a car and really explored, going into all the back roads and getting out every once in a while just to run and marvel at the fresh air, the hills, and the trees. We ran, screaming at the top of our voices, and we kept saying this country was for us because it was rugged, not manicured.

We had pulled into an overgrown dirt road to turn around when Peter said, "Hey, this house is empty."

With a spooky feeling, we peered into the windows. I was afraid someone would come jumping out at us, but no one did. The house was painted a barn red, and the best part was a shed in back. "I can turn that into a studio," I said, already figuring out where to build a kiln and seeing the shed freshly painted and fixed up with shelves for all the things I would need.

"I could make it bigger and turn it into a garage," was Peter's comment.

We almost had a fight. Studio, garage—garage, studio. . . . Then Peter had said, "We probably can't get it anyhow."

But we did. We rented it from the owner-farmer, who told us he had been going to fix it up for his son, but his daughter-in-law didn't want to live in the woods, so they'd moved to Albany. I don't think he believed we really wanted the place until we gave him a deposit.

The night before we left we had a great party. Peter and I made a huge pot of spaghetti and bought cases of beer and a gallon of red wine. We invited everyone we knew. Peter said he wasn't going to let me out on the street because I'd invite strangers.

I had wanted the party, wanted to see everyone, as if I were saying good-bye before a long journey. I guess I wanted our friends to reassure us that we were doing the right thing. But sometime in the middle of the evening, when the music was playing loud and everyone was talking, I suddenly wished they would go home. I didn't want to hear about Sam's interviews for jobs, or about the new apartment Judy had found, or the double bill at the Twenty-third Street movie house. I felt guilty because these were people I cared about, and I didn't want to feel that their conversation was unimportant. It wasn't. Sam's job was important; Judy's apartment was important. I felt terrible, as if I were wearing a mask with a fixed smile and an interested expression, but behind it was a different kind of face. Not bored, just out of it. The face of someone whose thoughts were a hundred miles away on a little red house, a shed, and woods. A whole different landscape.

The apartment was a mess, of course, when everyone finally left at two o'clock in the morning. "Let's clean up in the morning," I said to Peter. I was exhausted.

"No, let's do it now. I want to start off early tomorrow."

"But it's so late, and I'm so tired. We can get up early."

"You go to bed. I'll clean up."

Peter looked as tired as I felt. "I'll feel guilty. Besides, you're too compulsive."

"Go to bed," Peter ordered.

I stared at him for a minute, then went off. I could barely keep my eyes open. But something else had happened. I suddenly realized that I didn't have to do everything myself anymore. Peter was there. I could count on him. He was my friend. It was remarkable. I had dated some pretty odd characters, but I had fallen in love with Peter, and I hadn't even known that he was an exceptional human being. That kook, Katherine, had lucked out for sure.

3

"Don't you trust me?" Peter asked. The basket of mushrooms he held out to me looked poisonous, but I smiled and said, "Of course, I trust you. Except I'm not sure you know very much about mushrooms."

Peter washed one and ate it raw to prove to me that he wasn't out to kill us both. He had grown a beard, which made him look older than twenty, but very handsome. I watched Peter cook the mushrooms and felt like a fat cat.

We were having bucolic days. June in the country was an experience I hadn't known before. Everything was green, purple and white violets sprouted in the grass, irises that someone had planted in front of our door were blooming, and two chipmunks living somewhere under the house constantly chased each other about. One early morning we counted eleven different species of birds that came to the feeder Peter had made. Everything was new and beautiful. We walked in the woods, gathered dandelions and made salads, dipped, naked, in a nearby stream. We read, we lay in the sun and made love, and often did nothing except be lazy. Now June was turning into July, and we hadn't done anything sensible like fixing up the shed for my studio or making me a kiln. And we hadn't seriously looked for jobs, although our wedding money and our small savings were getting pretty slim.

"We have to go into town and market today," I said to Peter, after our lunch of mushrooms.

"Good. I want to stop and see the man I talked to over at the radio station about a job. He said to call him the beginning of July."

I looked at Peter with surprise. "I didn't know you'd talked to anyone."

"Well, I did. I phoned him a couple of weeks ago."

I was hurt that Peter hadn't mentioned it before. A stupid reaction. Of course, he had a right to call someone without telling me, but something big like a job. . . . "Is there an opening at the station?" I asked.

"There may be." He was standing in front of the mirror with his back to me, combing his hair, and he didn't turn around. Okay, so he didn't like to be questioned, and when he was ready he'd tell me. But I was dying to know more. I wondered why I didn't have a right to ask questions as much as he had a right not to offer information, but I kept my mouth shut.

We rode the twelve miles or so into Copake in the banged-up secondhand car we'd bought. I hated the idea of jobs. Not having to go to work had been so perfect, and the thought of Peter working for a radio station depressed me.

We stopped outside the village at a roadside place, where we bought vegetables, eggs, and chickens. "Only until we have our own," I said to Peter.

"One of these days," he answered vaguely, but I made up my mind that day to buy seeds and lettuce and tomato plants. Maybe later some chickens too, if Peter would put up a fence.

We didn't have a chance to talk about it then, because we ran into David Westley. David was our first friend up there. We'd met him in the market and felt at once that he was our kind. Not because he had a beard and wore jeans, but maybe because his voice was New York and his smile friendly. He was short and stocky and energetic, around thirty years old, a psychiatric social worker who worked in a mental-health clinic about fifteen miles away. He had sharp eyes, and he sometimes made me wonder if he was looking for our neuroses.

David greeted us warmly, and then said to Peter, "Did you see Ed Bates over at the radio station yet?"

"I'm stopping there today," Peter told him.

Another surprise for me. How could I be with a person twenty-four hours a day and not know some of the things he did? When had Peter talked to David about a job?

I was thinking about us as I picked out tomatoes, eggplant, summer squash, oranges, and grapefruits. Peter was probably more superstitious about discussing something before it happened than secretive. But I didn't like the idea, and I had to figure out why. I talked about being independent, but was that really what I wanted? Independence in terms of separate paths of thoughts and action? I was against phony togetherness, and I didn't want to be a clinging wife, but I liked to discuss things with Peter. But if he didn't want to discuss everything with me, I'd better face that fact. I wondered if I could talk to him about my disappointment, but then how can you discuss something with someone who doesn't want to discuss?

David interrupted my thoughts. "I told Angie Munson about you. She's looking for someone to work in her boutique over the summer."

"You're our guardian angel. Who's Angie Munson?"

"A nice lady. Another refugee from the city. She's from Philadelphia. She was widowed a couple of years ago and decided she wanted to start a different life, so she came up here and opened a boutique in the village. These woods are full of all sorts of weirdos."

"A boutique doesn't sound so weird to me."

"Maybe Angie isn't, but she has a weirdo of a nephew who's supposed to be working for her, except he's got a drinking problem. And then there are lots of others around: kids into religion, meditation, farming, artsy-craftsy stuff."

"Where do you see them, at the clinic?"

David laughed. "I see the healthy ones, the ones who have the sense to know they need help."

David's attitude annoyed me. "I thought people moved out to the country to do what they felt like doing. You put them down."

David started talking like a psychiatrist. "It takes strength to be yourself, to do your own thing, and a lot of these kids, and the older people too, just don't have it. They throw away their crutches before they've learned how to stand up."

I had a feeling David was trying to give me a warning, maybe to both of us, and I resented it. Peter and I knew what we were doing, and friendly as David was, I certainly didn't need him watchfully waiting for us to fall down. Furthermore, the last thing I wanted to do these beautiful summer days was to work in a boutique, but a job was a job and we had to eat. I felt as responsible as Peter about our venture, and getting jobs was part of it. Before I'd left home, my mother had said that if we needed money to let her know. But I had vowed then not to use her offer. We were on our own, and we had to be able to take care of ourselves.

After we finished our shopping, Peter and I agreed to find out about the jobs and meet in the village when we were finished. Peter dropped me off at the boutique and drove on to the radio station, which was out of town.

"Lots of luck," Peter said to me.

"I'm not sure I want the job."

He looked at me steadily with those clear blue eyes of his. "Don't take it then."

"I'll see. What about you? Do you really want to work in a radio station?"

"Of course. That's one of the reasons I picked this place. Because it has a radio station nearby."

Another piece of news. I thought we had picked

it because it was beautiful, and we'd found the house, and it was far away from the city, but still not a resort. Now I discovered that Peter had privately checked it out, probably at his school or at NBC. I suppose I should have been pleased that he was so practical—as Mom had said, one member of a couple has to be—but I was disturbed instead. As a matter of fact, I was mad, angry with Peter and angry with myself for feeling that way.

Angie Munson was a handsome gray-haired woman who seemed very efficient in a casual sort of way. I liked her. She said, "Do you have any experience?" Then she immediately added, "You don't need any here. You look attractive and bright, and we don't hard sell. We let people browse." That was obvious, for she wasn't paying the slightest attention to the customers in the shop except when one asked about prices and sizes. The shop had a little bit of everything: embroidered Indian blouses, slacks, jewelry from Mexico, pottery, caftans, leather belts, and jars of herbs.

"Do you mind working Saturdays?"

"It doesn't make any difference to me. We don't care about weekends."

"Who's we?"

"My husband and me."

I knew she was about to say that I looked too young to be married, but she didn't. A good mark for her.

We arranged money and time. I was to work Tuesday through Friday from one to seven, and Saturday from noon to six; she was closed on Monday. The hours were perfect. I felt very good and couldn't wait to tell Peter. Our move was going to work. I'd have my mornings to garden, to make pottery, to do what I wanted. Of course, I wasn't getting paid much, but we didn't need much money.

Peter hadn't fared as well. The man he was supposed to see wasn't there, but another person said they weren't ready yet to take someone on, and to get in touch again in a couple of weeks.

"It's just another job," I said. "Something else will turn up."

"Yeah. Driving a garbage truck. There's an ad in the local paper for a driver."

"What's wrong with that?" I asked. "Maybe you can do it part time."

We were driving home, and Peter gave me a swift, sidelong glance. "Because," he said, speaking clearly and vehemently, "I didn't come up to the country to drive a garbage truck."

I was silent for several minutes. We sure were on

different wavelengths that day. "I didn't think you'd care what you did for a job as long as we were able to do what we wanted to do."

Peter's voice was too gentle when he answered. "You don't understand. I told you that I want to work in a small radio station. That's my thing, what I'm interested in."

Then I said something mean. "You still want to be a big shot in a small pond."

Peter swerved out at a reckless angle and passed a truck before he answered. "I'll tell it to you all over again, and then I don't want to talk about it anymore. I came to New York because I wanted to work in radio and television. I sweated out two years of going to school and working to pay for it, and I discovered that New York was too much of a hassle, so I left with you. But that doesn't mean I still don't want to work in radio or television if I can find a small station. I want to work in my way and carry out my own ideas, not be another cog in a machine. I think I'll have a better chance in a small place. Do you understand?"

"Yes," I said meekly. And I did understand, except that I wasn't quite clear on how working for a small station was going to be less of a commitment to the commercial world that I thought we both wanted to get away from. My idea of living in the country had been to grow our own food, make things with our hands, be separate and independent of all the competitive, materialistic concerns most people were caught up in. I suppose I had had some private fantasy that once we were in the country, Peter would get into something like working with leather, or jewelry, or farming, or building us a house of our own. I even had a notion, which I hadn't mentioned to Peter, that if we grew our own food we wouldn't have to earn much money, and then we wouldn't have to pay any taxes. We could be free to live our own lives.

When we got home, I followed Peter up the path to our house, both of us loaded down with bags of groceries and the plants I had bought. The bright sun caught the red in his long, brown, curly hair, and he looked so strong and gorgeous that all my hostility faded away. He was my husband, and I loved him. He had to be himself—he had every right—and I would be an idiot to want him otherwise.

We spent the rest of the day digging up a square plot for a garden and putting in the seeds and lettuce and tomato plants. That night we cooked hamburgers outside and drank wine. Half laughingly I told him my idea of living off the land and making so little money that we could avoid paying taxes.

Peter roared. "No one in his right mind *chooses* to be poor," he said. "That would be really stupid. I don't believe in knocking myself out only to make money, but I want all the good things we can get. They're here, they exist, and we'd be dumb not to take our share. We're living in the twentieth century, darling. The whole idea is to share the wealth, for no one to be poor."

Of course, Peter made sense. He usually does, and I didn't argue with him, although I felt there was something beautiful about renouncing material possessions. Not because we couldn't get them, but because we didn't want them. But then I was romantic and unrealistic, and Peter was the practical one.

4

Leaving Peter at home to go to work was unpleasant. Not because I was the female and he the male—I didn't have that hang-up—but because being home was much more interesting. I discovered I really loved to cook; it was such fun to experiment, to throw things together and see what happened. And getting out in my shorts to dig in the garden was like being on vacation. Of course, staying home with Peter was the best part. We could talk or be silent, but always we were together.

Naturally there were bad days when Peter got restless and bored and terribly anxious about getting the job he wanted. He'd get very tense and disappear on long walks and stay away until I was frantic with worry that something had happened to him. When he returned he wasn't any better than when he'd left, and I'd just have to wait until his mood changed.

When he was in one of those moods, nothing was right. "This is the worst food I've ever tasted," he said to me one night.

"Well, it's all we've got, so we may as well eat it." I spoke in a stupid, cheerful voice. I'd made one of my leftover dishes, some ham and string beans and a little tired macaroni, not exactly gourmet but not awful either.

"You can eat it. I'll drink some milk." Peter pushed his plate away and took a quart of milk out of the refrigerator. It and the electricity were our pride and joy, our two modern conveniences. We had cold running water in the kitchen; hot water we had to heat on the wood stove. Peter spent a lot of time chopping wood. We talked about getting coal, but hadn't done so yet. There was a kind of bathroom with a sink and a peculiar rigged-up shower—cold water of course—and an outhouse. We weren't living in luxury, but I didn't mind.

"Come on, eat some. It's not that bad." I sounded like my mother, and I hated that awful, coaxing voice. So did Peter.

"Don't tell me what to do. You're so bossy. Anyway it's too late to eat. We never have supper before nine o'clock."

"I can't help it if I work until seven. What difference does it make when we eat?"

"All right point out that you're working and I'm not. I might have known you would sooner or later."

"That's an outrageous thing to say," I yelled at him. "You're the one who's furious that you're not working. I don't care if you never work, but you're the one who wants to do something *important*."

"You're damn right I do. You think I want to chop wood and live in a lousy shack the rest of my life. You talk about a 'fulfilled life,' but you're only thinking of your own fulfillment."

"Like working in a stupid boutique, I suppose."

"That was your choice."

It was our first real fight, and it was awful. We just yelled ourselves out and then shut up. The silence was worse than the yelling. Cold and hostile, we acted like people who hated each other. I was dying to touch him, to have him touch me, but I didn't know how to say I was sorry or if I was sorry. We went to bed without speaking. I couldn't fall asleep and was furious that Peter did.

In the morning he was an angel, acting as if nothing had happened. Except perhaps he did feel sorry because he said, "Let's go buy the bricks today, so I can get started on your kiln."

"That would be terrific." Not a word said about the night before.

I was thrilled about building the kiln. We had cleaned out the shed, painted it, and put up shelves. And on our walks I'd been keeping an eye out for places where I might find good clay. Though I wasn't a professional who knew all about mixing clay, I was willing to experiment. I figured that if primitive people had learned how to make pottery themselves, I could too.

Peter and I had figured out where to put the kiln next to the shed, and I had a book that showed how to build one. It is basically a simple outdoor oven. Peter, in his mysterious, efficient way, knew where to go to buy bricks. We bought a pile of beautiful yellow ones and bags of cement and sand, then arranged to have them delivered. I was so excited I didn't feel like going to work that day, but off I went.

"If you want to eat earlier," I said to Peter, "there's some meat and you could make a stew."

"Maybe I will. If I remember." We looked at each other and we both laughed. I kissed him good-bye.

But I was worried about Peter. What if he didn't get a job at the radio station? Eventually he'd have to do something. Peter wouldn't be happy staying around at home. I wasn't earning enough for us to live on when our savings were all gone, and we had very little left. Conceivably I could get a full-time job, but that wasn't what I had come to the country for. I was itching to get to my pottery.

Coming into the town and to the boutique was like entering another world from Peter's and mine. All those people, mostly middle-aged, wearing gorgeously tailored pants, tanned and manicured, the ladies' hair tinted in all shades. They spent their summers in the country, but never left the city behind. Some of the women came into the shop almost evrey day. They could as well have stayed home and spent their days in air-conditioned Saks Fifth Avenue. I guess some of the younger ones played tennis and went swimming, but I don't believe any of them went for a walk in the woods or noticed the beauty of the countryside.

Angie was a character, always in the middle of a crisis and, apologetically, leaving me alone in the shop. Today it was her nephew Dick again. "I don't know what to do with that boy," she said, greeting me and looking as if she hadn't slept all night. Probably she hadn't. "He came up to spend the summer with me, to help me in the shop, but all he does is drink. I'm worried sick about him. He didn't come home at all last night, and he has my car. I stayed up all night waiting for him. I don't know whether to call the police, or hospitals, or what."

Dick was twenty-two and, I thought, old enough to take care of himself. "He's probably okay. Sleeping it off someplace."

"He may be lying in a ditch for all I know." Angie was too upset to stay in the store and said she was going out in a friend's car to look for Dick.

It was Saturday and I didn't like being alone in the store, because it got really busy in the afternoon. The kids who came in were okay, but those rich women wanted everything in a hurry, although they weren't going anywhere except home to their swimming pools and cocktails. They took everything off the racks—sizes much too small for them—and never hung anything back. When I was alone on Saturday, I had to straighten out the mess and I never got out till way after six.

As I had expected, the place was hectic, and then suddenly around half past four the shop was empty. It wasn't going to last long, so I sat down, really tired, when Dick walked in. He looked bleary-eyed but otherwise okay.

"Where've you been? Your aunt's out looking for you. She's been worried sick."

"None of her business where I've been. I'm not a baby. I don't need her taking care of me."

"You had her car," I said, getting up to put away a pile of shirts left on a chair.

"So what? Big deal. She didn't need it. She gives me a pain." He was a tall, skinny boy with an unformed face, and he looked more like sixteen than twenty-two. The minute I'd cleared the chair, he sat down and stretched out his legs so that I had to walk around him.

"What'd you come up here for anyway?"

"I dunno. Nothing else to do. I couldn't stand my parents." He suddenly grinned, and his face looked rather nice. "A free summer, why not?"

"I thought you were supposed to work here." I was still walking around, putting things away.

"Yech. How can you stand all these old biddies and fags?" He looked up at me as though he were actually seeing me for the first time. "What are you doing here anyway?"

"Working. My husband and I wanted to get out of the city."

"Another nature lover. Back to the earth, I suppose. Listen, if you came here looking for peace and serenity, forget it. You won't find it."

"What makes you so sure?"

"Because I know." He thumped his head with his forefinger. "I'm not so dumb. I got brains, but I decided there's nothing to use them on. The whole world's going to blow up, so why bother."

I was wishing a customer would come in. Who needed this conversation on a sunny Saturday afternoon? Yet I didn't know how to get rid of him. He was looking at me intently. "Take my advice, just grab what you can. I'm out for everything I can get. It's the only thing that makes sense."

I didn't feel like arguing with him. "Why don't you take your aunt's car back to her?"

He stared at me, his little red eyes going up and down my figure. "I can't stand women like you," he said. "You're one of those strong kind I hate. Deliver me from self-sufficient women."

I felt like throwing something at him, but suddenly he decided to leave and staggered out of the store. Yet that stupid idiot had upset me. I wanted to be a strong person, but the minute a man used the word *strong* about a woman he made it sound like some hideous, evil blight. As if she had warts on her face and should be put away where she wouldn't offend anyone.

I thought of some of the women who came into the shop. Sometimes their husbands came with them, tired-looking men who were manipulated into working until they dropped dead of heart attacks. Still, those women weren't accused of being strong. Instead, they were treated like fragile porcelain that had to be cared for and kept beautiful. And at the other end of the spectrum was my mother. A lovely lady who'd taught her whole life in a poor school so that my father could do his thing. Because she was strong, she had the whole burden dumped on her. What I hoped for was in between. I didn't want to be taken care of, but I didn't want to be a martyr either. One partner didn't have to be stronger than the other. Why couldn't both be self-sufficient and independent and share the same risks?

I was exhausted when I closed the shop that night, but also excited to see how far Peter had gotten building my kiln. On and off I'd been thinking about it all day, and if we'd had a phone I know I would have called him a dozen times. We used the farmer's phone down the road for emergencies and important calls, but I couldn't very well consider my eagerness an emergency. I drove fast, but the ride home seemed twice as long as usual.

The first thing I saw when I came up the driveway was the pile of bricks and the bags of sand and cement left exactly where the truck had dumped them. I was wild. Nasty epithets and thoughts came hurling through my mind: mean, lazy, stinker . . . had nothing to do all day, wouldn't do something for me, just thinks of himself. . . . Then I panicked. Maybe something had happened to him. I ran into the house.

The stereo was turned up loud, and Peter was in

the kitchen very preoccupied over a boiling pot on the stove. "Hi, honey. We're celebrating tonight."

"What are we celebrating?" I tried to quiet my rising anger.

"I've got a job. Nothing sensational, but my foot's in at the radio station."

"Peter, that's fantastic. What happened? Tell me everything."

"Wait'll we sit down. I'm busy making dinner." That boy could be maddening sometimes. "Go take a shower while I get the food ready," he said.

I was dying of curiosity, but the scenario had to be his way. Keep your cool, girl, I told myself, it's his story.

Peter was not the speediest fellow in the kitchen. I took a shower, put on a long, cotton caftan Angie had given me, and sat outside until Peter called to tell me he was ready. He'd even put flowers on the table.

"Tell me, tell me."

Peter laughed. "How's the stew?" He was teasing me now as he heaped my plate and then his own.

"It's great." And it was very good. "Where'd you get the wine?"

"When I got a ride in with Henry to see about the job." Henry was our farmer-neighbor-landlord. Peter was going to talk at last. "They called me at

Henry's, and he came over to tell me to call them back. I did and Bates said to come see him. It's not much of a job, just a summer replacement, but it might lead to something." He was deliberately putting the job down, I could tell, but he was pleased and excited.

"So what is it? What will you be doing?"

"Running a dumb morning program, from eleven to one. Mainly announcing local events and interviewing local bigwigs and celebrities if any are around. Half an hour is for selling stuff people want to get rid of—old refrigerators, furniture, garden tools, puppies, anything. They have a few commercials. The guy who's been doing the program is pretty dumb. I think I can improve it."

"That's terrific. Two hours on the air. Can you fill it? I'd be scared stiff."

Peter laughed. "Trying to get everything in will be the problem. With a half hour for the selling, and station breaks and commercials, I've got around an hour and ten minutes. There are a million organizations around here, and they all want to be on the air with what they're doing. And I've got some ideas of my own."

He was really excited and I was happy for him. Everything was working out—our house in the woods, Peter's job, my part-time job. . . . Outside

I could see the pile of bricks for my kiln, and that was going to be working soon too. It was a happy, happy night.

5

Our life was falling into a routine. Peter went off to work quite early in the morning to get ready for his show. He had a lot of mail and notices to go through to get himself organized. He took the car because he had a distance to go. I either hitched a ride into the village or bicycled to the shop.

Peter was sorry he couldn't help me with the kiln. "But you can do it," he told me. "It's pretty easy." I didn't find it all that easy. Women's lib or no, there are some things a man can do more easily than a woman. At least, this woman. I'll grant that the reason undoubtedly is conditioning, but no one can change overnight. Finally I broke down and got Henry to help me, or rather I helped him, a little. When it was finished, the kiln was terrific.

I found a marvelous swampy place with really

good clay and was able to get started. Having a place to work that wasn't just a bedroom corner was wonderful. I even liked being alone, although at eleven o'clock every morning I turned on the radio Peter had rigged up for me in the shed so I could listen to his program. Hearing his voice come out of the box was weird. I thought he was very good.

After he'd been on the air a couple of weeks I could detect some of his touches. He would get in a crack about developers coming in with bulldozers and cutting down all the trees in order to put up rows of houses. He started going after the utility company that wanted to put in a new power line. His guests, I noticed, were people with liberal ideas, heavy on the side of conservation. The way he was able to work provocative ideas into an ordinary show was marvelous.

Peter and I were feeling good, so we decided to have a party. The idea was really Peter's, but I didn't mind. I'm not big on parties, and I was glad that we didn't know many people. "There's David Westley," I said, "and I suppose I should invite Angie. And there's Lucy and her husband Joe."

I had gotten friendly with Lucy at the shop, though I hadn't met her husband and Peter hadn't met either one of them. Lucy was a dark, thin girl, who gave guitar lessons and played and sang in a local coffee shop on weekends. She and Joe had come up from Brooklyn two years earlier and were trying to farm but still having a pretty rugged time. "We're getting it together," she would say, which gave me great encouragement. "If you both want it, you can do it," she once told me. "Joe and I work hard, but it's the way we want to live."

It's what Peter and I wanted too, I had told her, but doubts were crossing my mind.

"I'd like to ask some people from the station," Peter said, talking about the party, "but I'm not sure I want to ask them here." We were sitting in our kitchen-dining-living room, and Peter's glance around the room was disparaging.

"Where else would you ask them? What's wrong with this place?" I honestly didn't know what he was talking about.

"You'll have to admit it's pretty awful. The people at the station live in decent houses, with bathrooms and hot water. I can't picture Corinne going to an outhouse."

I felt hit with a cannonball. Corinne ran a really stupid early-morning show for women, telling them all the marvelous things they could do with corn-flakes and how to keep their kitchen shining and bright. I had never seen her, but I could tell from her saccharine voice what she was like—not a hair out of place. Probably she screamed at her children, if she was vulgar enough to have children, not to muddy the sacred floor.

"Corinne!" I shrieked. "I don't even want her in my house, let alone the outhouse."

"She happens to be a co-worker of mine," Peter said coldly. "If I invite Paul and Robert, which I certainly want to do, with their wives, I'm not going to leave Corinne out."

"But Peter, this is where you live. How can you be ashamed of it?"

"It's not that I'm ashamed of it," he said illogically, "but the place just isn't suitable for certain people."

"But if they're people worth inviting, then the kind of a house you have won't matter to them. I love this house, and I thought you did too."

"I don't believe you like all the inconveniences. They're a bore. I believe you don't have to ignore everything that makes life easier. As a matter of fact, I intend to put in a phone. It's ridiculous to have to rely on Henry's."

I felt as though he was giving me one blow after another. My mind never works fast in arguments. Peter was being so logical and speaking with such sure conviction that he confused me. Yet I knew there were flaws in what he was saying, from my point of view at least.

"I suppose it depends on where you want to spend your money," I finally said. "I don't find not having a phone such a hardship. I like to call my parents once in a while, which I can do from a pay phone in the village. It's just as easy and much cheaper. If we can save money, I'd rather give up the boutique and spend more time on my pottery."

"I thought you didn't believe in being supported by me." I could have punched the innocent, smug look on his face.

"But you like what you're doing and I don't. Besides, I think that if I work on my pottery, I'll be able to sell it and make money. I think Angie will take some in the shop if I really start producing. You don't have much faith in me, do you?"

The anger suddenly left Peter's face. "This is a stupid argument that will get us nowhere. A phone isn't that expensive. It's not going to make us or break us."

"And what about the party? Do you want to invite your friends or don't you?"

"I hope they'll be your friends too," he said kindly. "I'll think about it."

We left the matter there. But I kept thinking

about what we'd said and worrying. Peter could say things and then act as if he hadn't said them at all, although I knew that he hadn't forgotten.

I suppose I hadn't truly believed that Peter was all that dedicated to working in the media. I am not much of a newspaper reader, and truthfully radio and television bore me. It all seems like a lot of repetition of nothing, even the news, which is always full of disasters—fires, murders, wars, violence of one kind or another. Peter sometimes accused me of living with my head in the sand, but I could see no point in listening to a lot of horrible events I could do nothing about. It was my life, my only one, and I wanted it to be beautiful and serene. I wasn't looking for excitement. I wasn't asking for much. I was happy with my pottery, living with Peter, seeing a few friends, walking in the woods, cooking, making love. I had to think hard about Peter. I loved him so much. Maybe it was his vitality, his intensity and need to be involved, his restlessness that made him so attractive to a quiet person like myself. For the first time I worried about losing him. I wasn't afraid that something morbid would happen to him, but afraid that he would get bored with me. What if he discovered he needed someone more exciting, someone more ambitious for a luxurious and glamorous life?

I was the one who brought up the party again.

"I've been thinking," I said. We were sitting outside in the cool evening, watching the fireflies. "Let's have a country party on a Sunday. We can use those old boards in back and make a big table. It'll be like one of those scenes in a French movie with a peasant family sitting around a big table gorging themselves. I'll make bread and lots of chicken, and Lucy will give us all kinds of vegetables and salad, and we'll get a gallon of wine. Your friends from the station will think it's quaint."

We had one of those candle things going to keep away mosquitoes, and I could see Peter's face. He looked a little sceptical but agreeable. "That might be nice. If you really want to bother."

"It'll be fun. See what Sunday they can make it, and I'll ask Angie and Lucy. Also will you call David?"

On Tuesday we settled for the following Sunday, and I thought about the party all week. I wanted it to be beautiful, our first party in our own first home. Everything worked. The bread came out crusty and brown, the way we liked it. I made cookies and bought a watermelon that took up almost the whole refrigerator. Saturday morning I got a batch of fresh chickens from Henry and cooked them so we'd have them cold on Sunday.

We had a tremendous thunderstorm Saturday night, so Sunday was clear and cool. We set up the table outside and covered it with a pink cloth. The deep red roses from our one bush with the dark green paper plates I'd bought looked stunning on it. The paper plates had been a big decision, because Peter and I thought using them was wasteful. But we didn't have enough regular plates, so we made an exception for that once.

We had invited everyone for one o'clock, and Peter and I sat outside admiring each other and how pretty everything looked. He had on a clean blue work shirt and jeans, and I wore my long caftan.

Peter suddenly burst out laughing. "We look like an ad for a barbecue except there's no barbecue. I didn't realize you were such a domestic soul at heart."

"Do you mind?" I wasn't sure whether he was putting me on or not.

"No, I like it. You look as if I had insulted you."

"I guess I don't like the word *domestic*. It makes me think of women who empty ashtrays all day long."

"No danger of that." Peter laughed. He couldn't stand disorder and liked everything in its place, and I guess my untidiness bugged him. I leave my clothes around and let dishes and pots and pans pile up. I'm also a bit of a squirrel, collecting stuff I'll probably never use, like old jars and stones I pick up on the road. If Peter threw away a cup without a handle, I retrieved it much to his disgust.

By one thirty everyone had arrived. David came with Lucy and Joe. Joe was nice looking, with a big head of curly hair, a mustache, and very blue eyes. Lucy brought a huge bowl of potato salad and some baby carrots, zucchini, lettuce, and mustard greens from their garden for a vegetable salad. Angie arrived looking quite elegant, and to my dismay she had her nephew Dick with her. "I didn't think you'd mind," she said gaily. "The poor boy was going to be home alone all day."

"Oh no, it's fine," I said, lying as cheerfully as I could. I'd have to warn Peter to keep the wine bottle out of his reach.

Peter's friends came last. Paul and Robert with their wives, and Corinne. They drove up in an open sports car and looked terribly country club. Anne and Norma, the two wives, looked like twins in immaculate white pants and lots of gold chains hung over striped T-shirts. Corinne, who was around Angie's age, looked kind of crazy in a very short thing that belonged on a teen-ager.

As soon as everyone was introduced, Peter offered

drinks. My mysterious husband hadn't told me he'd bought vodka and tonic. The liquor turned out to be a good idea, because everyone loosened up and began to talk.

"This is an adorable place," Corinne said. "It must be marvelous living out here in the woods," she added, looking terrified of a bee that was buzzing over the food.

"We like it," I told her. "But we don't have any conveniences." I waved out back toward the outhouse, deciding I'd better let them know the worst right away.

"How quaint," Anne said, paling visibly.

Angie started asking Joe about his farm, which stirred quite a commotion, as if he'd revealed he was a snake charmer. "Do you really farm?" "How do you like it?" "What do you grow?" At least, Joe's farm kept the conversation going for a while. Being hostess to such a group wasn't easy for me. I felt there should be brilliant talk, witty and sophisticated, and so promptly became tongue-tied. Finally I stooped to exchanging recipes with Lucy. The food was very good, however, and it didn't matter too much that Peter sat and talked shop with Robert and Paul while the rest of us talked about nothing, and Dick drank wine.

I was getting drowsy from the heat and the wine,

and wishing that everyone would go home, when Dick suddenly came to life. "Say, Peter, that radio show of yours is pretty good. How do you get away with some of the stuff you're saying?"

First Peter looked startled, then wary. "I'm not getting away with anything. I don't know what you mean."

Dick roared. "Little innocent. I like that. But you're good. I like the little digs you manage to work in. It's about time someone talked sense on that station."

It was not the thing to say in front of Peter's immediate boss, Robert, the producer, and his assistant, Paul. "We think we put some pretty good programs on the air," Robert said, only mildly irritated.

"Good for what? Good for imbeciles." Dick laughed again, thinking what he said was pretty funny.

I was trying to figure out how to shut him up, when Angie got my distress signal and said, "Come on, Dick, time to go home."

But Dick was determined to deliver a monologue on the low-grade standards of radio and television, mouthing one cliché after another, and there was no shutting him up. His windup was the worst. "I'm afraid your days are numbered, chum," he said to Peter. "How can they advertise those exquisite condominiums, Pine Woods Estates, if you're going to make unpleasant cracks about developers wrecking the countryside." Dick shook his head sadly. "Surprised you've lasted this long."

There was a dead silence. Robert and Paul looked embarrassed; Peter was furious or in a state of shock, I wasn't sure which. And then David, bless him, started talking quickly about his mental clinic. But the party was finished. They stayed only a short while longer and then left. Angie managed to whisper to me that she was sorry, and of course I had to tell her she wasn't to blame. But I could have killed her for bringing that idiot nephew of hers along.

The minute everyone was gone, Peter turned on me in a rage. "Why in hell did you invite that stupid ass here?"

"I didn't invite him. I didn't know he was coming. Angie felt awful about him."

"She's as dumb as he is. I've been walking a tightrope at the station trying to slowly build up something good, and that half-wit has to come in with a sledgehammer. I could murder him. You don't give a damn if I lose the job. You'd be glad. You and your farmer friends don't approve of anyone working for what you call the Establishment.

But it's what I want, you understand! No, you don't understand." Peter banged his fist down on the table.

I was scared. Something that had been quietly festering underneath was now pouring out. The worst part was that in Peter's rage against me there was some truth. I really did wish that he didn't want to work in what to me was the dead end of the commercial world, but I had accepted his job and had been glad that he was finding a way to put something honest into it.

He had no right to say that I wanted him to lose the job, and I told him so, yelling.

Peter's face was grim. "You talk about people doing what they want to do, but you want me to do what you want. You may not want me to lose the job, but you'd love my doing something else. Something that fit into your scheme of what's important. To me this work is important, more important than making jewelry or leather goods and all the craft stuff that you worship."

"Like pottery?" I asked icily.

"Yes, like pottery too, if you want to know. I'm trying to reach people, to say something. You're making something for yourself, for your own pleasure."

"What a piggy thing to say. I happen to believe

that I can give a person pleasure with a beautiful object, more pleasure than listening to hours of nonsense on the radio in order to hear two minutes of what you can squeeze in."

We stood there glaring at each other. Then I started to cry, and Peter had his arms around me. "We sound so awful," I sobbed. "Like horrible people that I hate. Why do we say such terrible things to each other?"

"Because we don't agree on absolutely everything," Peter said soothingly, holding me tight. "And that's all right. Having a fight isn't the end of the world. We're both strong people with strong feelings and ideas. We're both yelling for equal time," he added, pushing my hair back from my face and kissing me. "If one of us isn't going to push the other around, as we swore we wouldn't, we're bound to push back sometimes. So long as one of us doesn't knuckle under we're okay."

"I hope so." I leaned back in his arms, exhausted. I wondered if others had to work so hard to hold on to what they believed, not to give up, not to yield because they loved someone a lot. You can compromise on the unimportant things, like who's going to wash the dishes, but when it comes to fundamentals you've got to be your own person. At least, Peter and I agreed on that.

6

Despite our kissing and making up, Peter remained tense. A few days later I asked him how things were going at the station, and he said fine. But I didn't believe him. He looked too wistful.

"I don't trust your producer, Robert. Nor Paul either for that matter," I said quite innocently.

Wow. Peter flared up. "How can you say such a thing? You don't even know them. They're behind me all the way. They like what I'm doing."

"That's what they tell you. I think they're waiting for you to hang yourself. Especially Robert. He has a sneaky look."

Peter got up from the table where we were sitting. "You and your feminine intuition. Baloney. You're the one who's waiting."

It was the same old argument. I didn't know how

to convince Peter that I didn't want him to lose the job. Not if he liked it and was able to put something of himself into it. But that didn't make me trust the men he was working for. I had seen Robert's narrow, smooth face when Dick had let loose at our party. He looked like someone who was tucking away information for further use, a use that wouldn't do Peter any good.

The shop had been slow that Wednesday afternoon, and Angie had let me go home early. I didn't want to get into another fight with Peter, so I went out to the shed to work. Going into that place was like entering a private cave, an oasis, where I felt integrated, a whole person, not someone being nibbled at by people and events. I felt safe there, with the clean, whitewashed walls and all my jars of minerals and colors clearly labeled. Peter with his mania for orderliness had set up everything for me, and out of gratitude to him I tried to keep it neat.

I had bought myself a wheel, and on the shelves a set of mugs, some odd bowls, and a pitcher were drying. But I still loved shaping the clay with my hands, without the wheel, and my prize piece was a large bowl, which I was building up little by little. I added to it every day, and it was taking on a rich mustardy, earth color. If the bowl turned out as I hoped, I was going to enter it with a few other things in a big craft show that Lucy had told me about. The show was in September in a nearby town, and Lucy said craft people came from all over to exhibit. She also advised me to make useful pieces for it, like mugs and pitchers and teapots, which I didn't mind doing, although I was fond of making odd shapes and experimenting with colors.

I had found some good red clay and was mucking it up to make some mugs for my mother. Twenty-second Street seemed so far away that I found it hard to remember how I had lived there with all the noise and commotion. I was so happy in our little house in the woods that I never wanted to leave it. I even hated more and more going into the village to the shop. When I was working in the shed, I could convince myself that my serenity ran deep, all the way through, solidly. Yet I knew there was a crack, that Peter, who was amiable and loving and comforting to lean on, was mysterious too and might do something unexpected at any time. That thought made me afraid.

When I went back to the house, Peter was outside doing something to the car. "I'm going down to Henry's to call up my parents," I said. "I'm making some mugs for my mother, and I'd like to ask them up for the weekend. That okay?"

Peter wiped his greasy hands on a rag. "Where'll they stay?"

"With us, of course."

Peter shook his head doubtfully. "It's an awful small house for four people. Where'll they sleep?"

"Don't you want them to come?" I loathed the edginess in my own voice.

"I'd like them to come. But where will they sleep?" His voice was calm.

"I thought we'd give them our bedroom. And we could sleep in the living room. You can have the sofa. I don't mind the folding cot."

"I'll sleep on the cot. Yes, ask them." But he was still frowning.

"What's the matter?"

"Nothing's the matter. I like your parents. I just don't think they'll be very comfortable here. I think you should get them a room in a motel."

"But that wouldn't be any fun. They won't mind for just one night."

"Okay, they're *your* parents."

Of course, Peter was the one who hated the inconveniences. So often he looked annoyed when he had to heat water to bathe, or when he went out at night to the outhouse. Now he had me worrying about whether my parents would enjoy spending a night with our makeshift arrangements.

Inviting my mother and father to come to my house was peculiar. Peculiar nice. We made a date for two weeks away. "We don't have any conveniences," I told my mother.

"We don't care. We just want to see you. You and Peter. Don't worry about us." Her voice was reassuring, and I felt better. Darling Peter didn't understand my parents. He was probably thinking of his own mother in Mason City, Iowa. She wouldn't like our house; she would hate it, the way Peter—no, I mustn't think that.

I ran home to Peter. He was lying in the string hammock we'd strung up between two trees, and I stretched out beside him and closed my eyes. He swung the hammock gently with one foot trailing on the ground, and, as always, his closeness, his arm around me, dissolved the fears. How in the world had I ever lived before, without Peter?

"Do you trust me?" he asked.

The question startled my drowsiness. "Of course, I trust you. What a question. How do you mean?"

"I don't mean about other women. I love you. I don't even look at anyone else. I mean trust me, my judgment—me, a person."

"I trust you like I'd trust my own husband," I said flippantly. But the question troubled me, and soon I had to get up because the swinging hammock was making me dizzy.

I was getting used to Peter's moods; he could suddenly become tense and remote, then bounce back, warm and loving. Lucy kept telling me, "I'm sure his moods have nothing to do with you. Just remember that they're not your fault, so you don't have to get worried and feel guilty. It's the way he's made, that's all."

Lucy and I were becoming very close. I loved her. She was sensible and calm, but not smug or stuffy. She and Joe had two little boys, four and two, and I thought they had a wonderful life. They never fussed about the kids, making them eat when they didn't want to or go to bed if they weren't sleepy. Joe took care of the children more than Lucy did, since he was home when she went out to give her guitar lessons or played on weekends. Lucy said that in the winter Joe picked up odd jobs, carpentry and such, and she stayed home more, so things evened out.

I was living in a cocoon. The weather was beautiful. Every day I gathered lettuce and greens from my garden—the tomatoes were ripening—and I could pick our own beans and squash too. I was getting excited about my parents coming up. I wanted to show them how well we were living, how everything was working.

The Thursday before they were due, the boom

fell. When I came home from work, Peter was in a terrible state. I thought something awful had happened from the look on his face. He was lying in the hammock, but he was far from relaxed. He looked angry, tense, and hurt too. I started to put my arms around him, but he turned away, as if he couldn't bear any sympathy.

"What is it? What happened?"

"I quit the job."

Relief must have flooded my face—no one was dying; no one had been killed. The late afternoon sun was still shining, throwing a shaft of light across our house that lighted up the windows with a special beauty.

"You quit? You weren't fired," I said tentatively, thinking that if you do something yourself it's not as bad as something that is done to you.

"I quit before I got fired. The dumb bastards."

"What happened?" I was aching to comfort him, but I couldn't say it was only a job and he'd get another one. Something deeper than the job was burning him up.

"That idiot Dick started it. Right after that Bob started fussing about the show. I mustn't say this, and I mustn't say that. Then he had Paul writing scripts for me. If you'd been listening to the show you'd have heard how stupid it was."

I felt awful. I hadn't been listening; I'd been

so involved with my pottery I hadn't turned on the radio. I'd been a terrible wife, but of course my listening wouldn't have done any good, wouldn't have changed anything.

"I couldn't take it any longer. They were going to fire me anyway. So I quit. I wasn't going to be a dumb voice for Paul's gibberish."

"I guess you can't do anything really independent on radio. Or television either, as my father can tell you."

"I don't believe that," Peter said angrily. "I'm not giving up, not yet. There's public educational television, and there are some good newscasters. One day I'm going to have my own news show, you'll see."

"Is that what you meant when you asked did I trust you?"

Peter gave me a sharp look. "Yes. You've got to have confidence in me. You've got to believe the way I do. I need you, Katie—I know I'm sometimes pigheaded and selfish, but this is important to me. Outside of loving you, it's the most important thing in the world. I think I can make it, and I'm going to break my back trying. I want to tell people the truth, not just sell them soap and little houses. I think people are getting wise, and there's a place for someone like me who's willing to stick his neck out."

His eyes were bright and his face flushed. He was beautiful, but his intensity frightened me. I felt so inadequate, as if I'd been living with a superior person whom I hardly knew and who expected something of me that I wasn't at all sure I could give. My own plans for living seemed so pitiful compared to his. I wasn't ambitious or smart enough to want to change things. I felt almost ashamed of how little I wanted, how content I was to make my pottery, to work in the garden, to have a house of my own, to love Peter. . . . His eyes were on a star so much bigger and brighter than mine.

He frightened me because he made me think of my father. What if Peter didn't make it? What if he didn't find that ideal spot he was looking for, but got bruised and hurt instead, like my father, over and over again? And I thought of my mother too; she had sacrificed her life for her husband's dreams. I could remember all the nights she had come home from school so tired, wishing she could quit and do something else. She would have liked to study singing—she had a lovely voice—but you can't have two artists in a family, she would say with a wistful smile, neither one with a steady salary. Teaching brought in a regular paycheck, and she was the one who was stuck.

I didn't want to do what she had done.

I said nothing of this to Peter, but inside I was seething with rage. Not with Peter, but with the stupid, cockeyed world that wouldn't leave us alone in peace.

"Listen, Katie," Peter was saying, "I'm going to talk to your father about a job in New York."

I was stunned. "But we haven't given this a chance." I was sitting on the grass beside the hammock, looking at the way the sun had moved down from the windows, leaving them in shadow, and was now turning the wild lilies into a blaze of brilliant orange. "Not New York, Peter. You haven't even looked for anything else around here."

He got up from the hammock and stood over me. "You refuse to understand. I don't want *anything*. Just listen to me. Back in Mason City I worked hard to get to New York. I mowed lawns, I ran a garbage truck, I did haying, anything I could to get some money. When I got to New York, I went to school and worked at the same time. Edward Murrow was my hero. He went to every part of the world to dig out what was happening. The two guys, Bernstein and Woodward, did it for the *Washington Post* on Watergate, and they weren't much older than I am. I want to do the same thing on television. I got scared in New York. I felt like a lost peanut, and I thought a small station would be better. I was wrong. At least, I'm not afraid of mistakes, but I don't have to keep on living with them. And in a funny way this job has given me confidence. What I did was good—I know it was good—and those goons know it was good or they wouldn't have stopped me. Now I've got to find a way to do what I want. Maybe I'll have to do some silly shows for a while, but I can keep my eyes open and make contacts. Now I'm ready for television and New York. There's no other place. Honey, you've got to understand. I'm going to be big some-day, and when you're big you can be free."

As I listened silently to every word he said, I felt a tremendous surge of pride. I hadn't made a mis-take. Peter was great. But why did I feel so sad? Sad, and ashamed of my sadness. I thought an astro-naut's wife must feel this way when she sees her husband go off into space, leaving her alone on old-fashioned, plain earth, wondering if the mission is worth it, worrying if he'll come back, wishing per-haps that she had married someone ordinary who'd be content to putter around the house.

And I thought, treacherously, maybe my father will discourage him, tell him that no one can escape the corruption. . . . I was crazy. My father would grab hold of Peter's dream as if it were his own. He'd have a million suggestions and do everything he could to help him. My next wild idea was to call my mother and tell them not to come. But why disappoint them, and besides, what difference would it make? Peter would go to New York anyway.

The sun had disappeared now behind the big hill where I went picking berries, and I was sitting in shadow. I don't want to go to New York; I don't want to go to New York. Then I said the words out loud, "I don't want to go to New York."

Peter answered quickly, "Of course, you don't." He laughed. "I'm not about to compete with your kiln and your tomatoes. First I have to get a job anyway, but I'll be able to get up here a lot. I like it here. I'm not as mad for this house as you are, but if I start making money maybe you won't mind some conveniences. Anyway we'll worry about that when we come to it. Honey, don't look so forlorn. I'm not deserting you. I don't know why we can't each have what we want."

"And still be together," I added.

"And still be together," Peter said.

When we went in to make supper, I tried to kick my depression. I wanted to celebrate with Peter, share his excitement and confidence. I don't know if I succeeded. Peter was wound up; he talked and talked and I listened. When we went to bed I still felt sad inside, and I clung to him. We made love passionately, as if there were no tomorrow and we were never going to see each other again, which was the way I felt. "Katherine, darling, I'm glad you're my wife," Peter said.

"And I'm glad you're my husband."

I fell asleep, exhausted, but I woke up later from a nightmare. I couldn't remember it, but I knew that in my dream I'd been terrified. Our room was bathed in moonlight and for a long time I looked at Peter, sleeping peacefully, before I fell asleep again.

7

My parents were darling. They came laden with goodies—a huge steak, Dad's Scotch, cheeses, my favorite expensive pistachio nuts. And they didn't put down the house for a second—everything was lovely, everything was great. We drove them into the village on Saturday—good Angie had let me take the day off. Mom bought slacks and a blouse in the shop, Dad bought jeans in a funny, dusty, old store where Peter got his. We all had ice-cream cones, and when we got home we took them for a walk in the woods.

We sat outside while Peter cooked the steak on the outside grill he had set up. Everything was beautiful until we sat down to eat. Then Peter started talking about his plans, and I got a nervous stomach. Dad's reaction was exactly as I had privately predicted it would be. "I knew this was no place for you," he said to Peter. "You've got talent, and the city's where you can get paid what it's worth. I'm glad you found it out so soon."

"It's not the money," Peter said, "although I don't object to money. It's finding a spot where I can have a chance to do what I believe in. I think there's a revolution happening, and people honestly want to improve the quality of their lives."

My father agreed. "You're absolutely right. I've been in this business a long time, but I still believe in people. Madison Avenue's going to have to learn they can't get away with phoniness anymore."

They went on talking, the two of them, building each other up to the sky. My mother turned to me. "Does Peter plan to do this right away?" When I nodded my head, she said, "You know you can stay with us until you find an apartment. Your room's there."

"Maybe Peter will use it. I'm staying here."

My sweet mother, who thought she was with it, was shocked. "You should be where your husband is. If he has to go to New York to work, you have to go too. Besides, you can't stay here alone."

"Of course, I can stay here. Peter isn't going to live in New York. He'll stay in when he has to, *if* he gets a job. He'll be out here a lot." We were both speaking in low voices, underneath the men's conversation.

My mother shook her head. "You're making a mistake. I don't often try to give you advice, but a wife belongs with her husband. For your own good too, Katherine. A man can get lonesome by himself, especially at night in a city like New York."

I had to laugh. "Honestly, Mom. I'm not worried about Peter chasing around. Anyway, if he wants another girl, he can have one."

"You wouldn't mind?" She looked at me with disbelief.

I thought a minute. "I suppose I would, but I wouldn't stop him. What good would it do?"

"You don't have to give him the opportunity," she said crisply.

It was a crazy conversation that I did not want to pursue. I didn't like talking about Peter and myself with my mother. In spite of her self-image as a "progressive," she had very conventional ideas about love and marriage, as she showed in her attitude to my father and the way she catered to him. Sometimes her behavior got on my nerves, especially now that I was married myself. She always put him first, giving him the best part of the meat, the most comfortable chair, waiting on him as if he couldn't do anything for himself. The thought occurred to me that my father had never cooked a meal or washed the dishes or done the marketing at any time that I could remember. I was sure that she'd say those chores were her job, even though she worked as hard as he, if not harder.

That night when Peter stretched out on the cot beside me, on the sofa, he said, "I think I'll go back to the city with your folks tomorrow. Your father has some ideas, and I can get an early start Monday morning."

I felt numb. "You're really in a hurry, aren't you?"

"What's the sense of hanging around?" After a few minutes of silence, he said, "You're not with me on this, are you?"

"I don't know. I guess I've got to get used to the idea. I'm a slow learner. Everything's happening too fast."

"I wish you understood," Peter said.

"It's not difficult. You want to go one way and I another," I told him in a desolate voice.

Peter gave a deep sigh. "You're making a big thing out of nothing. We're not going different ways. We always said we each had to do our own thing, didn't we?"

"I guess I never thought our interests would take us in different directions. My big thing is that I love you, and I assume you love me, and to me that means living together. In the same place."

"You can come to the city with me."

I wanted to say, "And you can stay in the country," but I didn't. "It'll be all right," I said. I didn't want to talk anymore. But I still had that awful depressed feeling that the geography was only the beginning—the beginning of losing Peter.

I hated that Sunday. It was a hot, muggy day, and just as I was about to fix lunch we had a thunderstorm and the power went off. Everyone was very cheerful except me, saying weren't we lucky to have a wood stove. All day I had the weird feeling that my parents and Peter were in one place, and I in another. As though he were their son and I the outsider. Peter and my father drove into the village to get the Sunday papers, leaving Mom and me alone, and I was sure she was going to talk about things I didn't want to talk about.

I was right. "Are you and Peter getting along all right?" she asked. "I don't want to pry," she added hurriedly, "but you seem pretty tense."

"We've been getting along fine. I guess I'm not crazy about his going to New York," I said, immediately wishing I hadn't. Then, suddenly, much to my disgust, I burst into tears, the last thing in the world I wanted to do in front of Mom.

She was all mother, soothing and sympathetic,

murmuring pat phrases. I'd probably been working too hard and not eating right. If Peter and I loved each other, everything would all work out.

"Don't mind me," I said, wiping my face, "I'm kind of edgy. It's nothing."

I didn't get any less edgy as the day wore on. I wanted to die when Peter hauled out a suitcase and packed some clothes. "You planning to stay away a year?" I asked, as he stuffed the bag with shirts and underwear.

"It's hot in New York and I sweat," he said grumpily. Then he looked up and saw my face. "Look, darling, it's not a funeral. If you don't want me to go, say so. I'll stay here and drive a damned garbage truck."

"Don't be ridiculous," I mumbled. Then we grabbed hold of each other and held each other tight. I was behaving like an idiot, like some sappy, weak sister, not the strong, independent girl I imagined myself to be. I muttered something to that effect to Peter, and he howled.

"Save me from strong women. Of course, you're an emotional female, and that's why I love you. One good reason anyway."

"Pig," I said, and immediately felt a little better.

But when he was dressed in his city, looking-for-a-job clothes he seemed a stranger.

I was almost relieved when the three of them got on the six o'clock bus to New York. I stood waving to Peter and making silly faces until the bus pulled away. Then I got into the car and drove home.

I spent the most horrible evening of my life. The thunderstorm hadn't cleared the air one bit; it was still hot and sticky, and the house was terribly empty. I'd been alone there plenty of times, but I had never felt lonesome before.

I wanted to stay inside, but the house was too spooky. Everything looked so sad—Peter's jeans hung up neatly the way he kept them, his magazines, the book he'd been reading left open on a table, the zany posters he'd put up on the wall, especially his favorite of a huge, pathetic ape with a baby ape in her lap. If I was so lonesome already, how was I going to get through the night alone in our big double bed?

I went outside and got bitten to death by bugs and came inside. The power had come back on, and I thought about going out to the shed to work, but I didn't even feel like doing that. I just sat and moped.

Suddenly I wished we had a telephone. I could call Lucy and talk to her. The more I thought about it, the more I thought I'd go crazy if I didn't have someone to talk to. I could have gotten into the car and driven over to Lucy and Joe's, but I felt too miserable to be social.

Finally I made myself a sandwich and went to bed with a spooky mystery story. It was the wrong thing to do. I kept hearing noises, creaky sounds, thinking I heard footsteps, working myself up into a fury with Peter for having left me. Every single old-fashioned notion about love came to my mind, all of them adding up to the conviction that if Peter really loved me, he wouldn't have gone to New York and left me there alone. Some small, rational part of me said, if that's the case, then if you loved him, you would have gone with him.

I finally fell asleep silently screaming. Peter and I didn't measure love that way . . . our love was different. We were separate persons, with separate needs and identities. I did not want to be a whimpering wife.

The first thing Monday morning I went down to Henry's house and called the phone company to have a telephone installed. It was going to be expensive but not too bad, since the pole was already there for Henry's phone. I had capitulated, but I didn't want to be a martyr to my own pigheadedness. Besides, it would make Peter happy. Afterward I felt very sensible and grownup, furious that they couldn't install the phone immediately instead of "sometime in the next several days."

I started out being very good that morning. I went to work on my pottery, telling myself that the day was no different from any other morning when Peter was at the radio station. But it *was* different. I couldn't turn on the radio and hear him, and I kept wondering what he was doing now. And what was I doing here, alone in the woods, making mugs and bowls that no one would ever want to buy? Then I worked at the wheel, and my heart stopped beating so fast. When I got tired, I went outside and stretched out flat on my back on the grass. It was so quiet and beautiful and peaceful that I felt my strength coming back. Peter and I loved each other, and we would make the new arrangement work. Who said we had to have a conventional marriage, seeing each other every day, having every meal together? This way we would never get bored with each other, we'd always have something to bring back, to talk about. . . . I did a great job on myself.

Later, at the shop, even Angie couldn't break me down. I told her about Peter going to New York to look for a job, and she was as horrified as my mother. "You're making a terrible mistake," she said. "A wife belongs with her husband." The exact words my mother had used. "I've been around a lot longer than you have, and, believe me, every successful man has a wife behind him in the wings to back him up. Peter needs you. Looking for a job is no fun, and even when he gets one, it's not going to be easy. If you want him to get ahead, to be a success, you have to stick right along with him."

"But I didn't marry Peter because I wanted him to be a success. Not the way you think of success. We wanted to have a different kind of life, to live in the country, to enjoy ourselves, not to make money."

"You're being very childish," Angie said. "Every man wants to make money. That's what counts. You'll change your mind. You'll get tired of living in that shack of yours with no hot water, no bathroom. It's ridiculous, Katherine, and you know it."

"I don't know any such thing," I yelled at her. "I'm happy there. I don't want to spend my life working for conveniences. They get broken all the time anyway. I don't want to live to buy, and I don't think Peter really wants to either."

Angie gave up, shaking her head, but I didn't care. Why couldn't people understand that Peter and I had ideas for a *different* kind of life.

Lucy and Joe would understand, and I went to

see them that night after work. They had bought an old barn that they were gradually converting into a house. So far it was primitive, like ours, but what they had done was beautiful. They had one huge room in which they worked, ate, and slept, with a small section partitioned off where the boys slept. Joe had used barn siding for the interior wall, and a good section of the barn had a cathedral ceiling. The kids played upstairs in the hayloft, which would eventually be made into bedrooms. It would be a terrific house someday.

Lucy was practical and wonderful. "You have to be patient," she said, "and give Peter time. He's been going back and forth as though he doesn't know yet what he wants to do."

"He wants to work in television, that's pretty clear," I told her.

"I know. That's what he says. But he got disillusioned with the city and the big networks once, and he may again. He may be looking for something that doesn't exist, a place where he can do what he wants, regardless of the big brass and the sponsors. You have to sit tight and wait. He's got to find out for himself."

"And what if he does find out? Then what? That doesn't mean he'll find something out here that he wants."

"Peter's pretty sensible. He's idealistic up to a point. He'll figure out that if he's got to compromise on the job, he would be happier here than in the city. If he can't get what he wants in TV, he may decide that he wants to do something entirely different."

"Like what?"

"I don't know. Maybe farm, the way we're doing."

"I don't think Peter would like that. Besides, I think he's going to find what he wants."

"Is that what you're afraid of?" Lucy asked with a smile.

"I guess I am," I admitted. "I'm afraid he's going to find it in the city."

"Then what will you do?"

"That's the big question. It isn't only the city—it's a whole way of life. We started out both wanting the same thing, and now I'm not so sure."

"You're too impatient," Lucy said. "He only left yesterday, and you're already worrying about what's going to happen. Relax, take it easy and wait."

Easy words, *take it easy and wait*. The trouble was I didn't know what I was waiting for. Part of me wanted Peter to get what he wanted. I loved him, and he should be happy at what he'd be spending a good part of his life doing. But I couldn't shake the awful foreboding fear that if he was successful, something terrible would happen to us.

I waited until Tuesday night to telephone him, using a pay phone in the village. Of course, nothing had happened yet, but he sounded cheerful. He said he was going to stay in the city through Friday and then come up on the bus. I was to meet him at six o'clock at the bus station.

"I miss you," Peter said.

"I miss you too."

I felt very alone after I hung up and drove home.

8

On Wednesday morning I woke up feeling really sick to my stomach. I'd probably picked up a bug, I decided, and made myself a cup of tea. When I sat down to drink it, a thought suddenly hit me. Maybe I was pregnant. My period was around three weeks late, but I had been late occasionally before, so I hadn't paid any attention. The idea was so exciting that I didn't know what to do. I wished Peter were there. I wished the phone were in so that I could call him, but that would be silly until I was sure.

No, it must be a bug. But maybe I *was* pregnant. . . . My thoughts went back and forth like a Ping-Pong ball. I was still sitting there with the cup of tea, which I could barely get down, feeling sick and elated at the same time, when the telephone men arrived. I welcomed them as if they were old friends. They were lovely and worked quickly and efficiently, and when they were finished, the bright, shiny telephone looked quite silly on the wall of our makeshift kitchen. Yet I loved it, because I could pick up the receiver and talk to Peter whenever I wanted.

Still, I restrained myself from calling him the minute the telephone men left. I called up Lucy instead. "My first call on my new phone," I said.

"Even before Peter?"

"Yes." And I told her why. She was as excited as I was.

"You'd better go see my doctor. You'll like him, and he'll let you have natural childbirth. You want that, don't you?"

"I don't know. Yes, sure, I guess so. I don't know much about it. I'm too excited to think, and I'll have to talk to Peter about it."

Lucy said she'd call Dr. Farnum and try to get an appointment for that day after work. He had office hours from seven to eight in the evening right in the village, and I could see him after work.

"Do you think it's all right for me to ride my bike into town?" I asked.

"Of course. Why not? You've been riding it, haven't you?"

"I wanted to make sure." Though I had the car, I liked the bike ride.

The idea of a baby growing inside of me was exhilarating. I didn't think I could get through the day until I knew for sure and could talk to Peter.

Lucy called back to say I could see the doctor at seven fifteen and offered to pick me up and drive me home after my appointment. I didn't do very much that morning. As a matter of fact, I spent a good deal of it sitting and looking at Peter's poster of the ape with the baby ape in her lap. That crazy ape had a wise, knowing, and content expression on her face, proud and protective too in the way she was shielding her baby with her ape hands. I was already in love with my baby even before I knew I was having one.

I was very good about not saying a word to Angie, and fortunately we were so busy that there wasn't much time to talk.

I left the shop promptly at seven and walked down the street to Dr. Farnum's office. It was above the drugstore and reached by a tiny, automatic elevator. There were two other doctors' offices on the floor, and the joint waiting room was jammed. I had to wait a half hour before the nurse called my name.

Dr. Farnum, a pleasant man in his mid-fifties,

was obviously a very busy doctor and quite businesslike. He asked me a number of questions, jotted my answers down on a card, took my blood pressure, which was normal, and then motioned me into a room for the examination.

I was pretty nervous by this time and very relieved when the examination was over and he told me to get dressed. "You probably are pregnant," he said, "but I can't be absolutely sure. We'll take the pregnancy test."

When I left, he told me to call him around one o'clock on Friday.

"But do you think I am?" I asked him, pleadingly.

He gave me a quick smile. "I think so, but don't count on it until we get the results."

The letdown was awful, and I was mad at the whole medical profession for not being able to tell a woman whether or not she was having a baby. What did they go to school for all those years, if they didn't know something that simple?

Lucy was waiting for me, and I let off my steam on her. She thought I was pretty funny. We picked up my bike and put it on her car rack, and she drove me home. I made a sandwich for myself, and we sat down and talked. Lucy asked me what I was going to do if I was pregnant.

"What do you mean? Have the baby, of course. I'm so excited about it."

"Of course, you'll have it. I mean about Peter being in New York and you up here."

"I haven't even thought about that." Just thinking about the baby had filled my mind all day. "I don't suppose I'll do anything."

"It could be a reason to ask him to stick around," Lucy said tentatively.

I looked at her and our eyes met. Then I shook my head. "No, that would be lousy. You wouldn't do that, would you?"

"I don't think so, but you seemed so upset . . . I just thought you might."

"No." Then I had a frightening thought. "You don't suppose that Peter will think that's why I suddenly got pregnant, do you?"

Lucy laughed. "Of course not, silly. If you *are* pregnant, it happened weeks ago, before Peter ever thought about going to New York."

I poured us some coffee. "It's funny, but if I am pregnant, I might mind less if he has to be gone a few days each week. I won't feel so alone . . . having a part of him here with me. I don't mean as a hold on him," I added vehemently. "But we'll be more of a family, have something more solid." I patted my belly and laughed. "There's nothing very solid there yet."

"Peter may want you to be with him in the city," Lucy suggested.

"It's healthier here. But we'll see—the whole thing may turn out to be nothing at all."

We talked on and on, and Lucy told me all about natural childbirth and how wonderful she thought it was, while I kept thinking the whole thing was something I was imagining. On Friday the doctor would surely tell me that it was a false alarm.

When Lucy left, I had to telephone Peter. I could not resist that shiny new phone. My mother answered and told me that he was out. "I think he's over at Sam Levine's," she said. "We really don't see much of him. He's been very busy."

"Has anything happened about a job?"

"I don't think anything definite. He'll tell you himself. Are you all right? You sound excited."

"I'm fine. I'm not excited," I lied. We talked for a few minutes, then I gave her our new telephone number and said good-bye before I was tempted to say anything to her. Not reaching Peter was a letdown, and the house was terribly lonesome. When I walked to the outhouse in the dark, I wondered if I was cuckoo to stay there alone while Peter was probably having a wonderful time in New York with his friends.

*　　*　　*

My hand was actually shaking when I dialed Dr. Farnum's number exactly at one o'clock on Friday from Angie's shop. Of course, the line was busy. He had probably told twenty other people to call him at the same time, I thought with disgust. After about five tries, I finally reached him. "A positive result," he said calmly. "You are pregnant. Watch your diet, don't gain too much weight, and come to see me in a month." As if he were telling me it was going to be cloudy with showers the next day, yet he was giving me the most important news of my whole life.

I ran to Angie and threw my arms around her. "I'm going to have a baby! Can you believe it?"

"It's happened before," Angie said with her wry smile. But she was darling and sent out for a nice lunch to celebrate. I decided not to call my mother until after I'd told Peter. Getting through that afternoon, waiting for six o'clock to meet Peter, seemed endless.

As usual the bus was late, and when it finally arrived my polite Peter let all the ladies get off first. It was wonderful to see him. I felt as if he'd been gone for weeks. He looked great. "Your mother's cooking," he said.

"What happened? Tell me everything," I said, when we were in the car. I was holding back on my news until we got home.

Peter grinned. "I got a job."

"That's terrific." I honestly meant it, but at the same time my heart fell. "What, what?"

"It's not much, and I don't know absolutely yet, but I'm pretty sure I'll get it. It's as an assistant producer, which sounds good but pays peanuts. With NET—that's the important thing. At least, I have an in where I want to be. It's a half-hour interview show. I'll have to do some screening of people and digging up background material. It's more research than anything. For instance, if a politician is to be interviewed, I have to dig up everything he ever said—that kind of stuff."

"Fabulous. It's what you want, isn't it? I mean the experience will be tremendous. It's great that you got something so fast."

"I was lucky, at the right place at the right time. I had a couple of interviews, and I still have to be okayed by the top guy, but I think they liked me. Quitting the job up here, and why, didn't hurt me any with them. I told them the truth."

We were almost home when I asked the question that had been uppermost in my mind. "Will you have to be in the city all week?"

"The show's Friday night. It'll depend. Maybe sometimes I will. I can certainly come out Friday night after the show—it's on seven thirty to eight—so I could get here around ten. And I should be able to stay until Tuesday afternoon or maybe Wednesday morning, which won't be too bad."

My spirits soared. "That would be marvelous. If you have to stay in only on Wednesday and Thursday nights, that's nothing at all."

"Don't count on it every week," Peter said cautiously. "Some shows are going to take more work than others."

"Yes, of course." I was so happy. When we got out of the car, we stood and hugged each other the way we couldn't at the bus station.

I had splurged on a steak and wine for dinner, and after Peter had showered and we were sitting down, sipping our wine, I said, "I have some news too."

"What?" Peter asked.

I looked directly into his eyes. "I . . . we're going to have a baby."

Peter stared at me. He was really stunned. "You're kidding."

I shook my head. "I am not. I saw Dr. Farnum, Lucy's doctor, and had the pregnancy test and everything. It's for sure." I was in a panic. The thought had never occurred to me that Peter might not be as happy as I about our baby. But then I saw that he couldn't absorb the news. He kept looking at me with wonder as if I were some strange creature he had never seen before. Finally his face broke into a wide grin.

"I'll be damned," he said. He jumped up wildly from the table and threw his arms around me. "We're going to have a baby. We're going to have a baby," he sang at the top of his voice, dancing around like a nut.

Then he downed a glass of wine in one gulp, sat down, and looked at me soberly. "It's the craziest thing I ever heard of. It's scary."

"I'm not scared. Lucy told me all about natural childbirth. You can be there with me when it happens. We'll both see the baby being born."

Peter looked even more frightened. "I wasn't thinking of that part, although it sounds pretty scary too. I mean the idea of a baby, of being a father. I'm not ready. I don't feel finished. We're still such kids."

"I guess if we're old enough to be married, we're old enough to have a baby." I put my arms around him. "Don't be scared. We'll be beautiful parents. Look at Lucy and Joe. They're young, and they have two kids. I think it's good to be young. We'll be closer to our kids."

Peter laughed. "Don't say *kids*. One's enough for a long time."

*   *   *

We had a peculiar weekend, full of love and an inner excitement. Doing the ordinary chores like cooking and washing was hard. I wanted to do nothing but lie in the hammock and dream.

Saying good-bye to Peter on Sunday night was the hardest. "Call me the minute you know about the job," I said.

"Yes, of course. And listen, take care of yourself, and our baby. Don't do anything silly."

When I drove back to the house alone, I tried to hang on to all the good feelings of the weekend. Everything was going to be all right. But the fine words I had said to Lucy about feeling less lonesome because of the baby vanished. I felt more lonesome than ever.

9

In September the leaves started to turn, and the evenings were beautifully cool. The country was absolutely gorgeous, which was more than I could say of my life. I felt mixed up. I was playing so many different roles that I was losing sight of who I really was.

Peter got his job and left my mother's apartment to move in with his friend Sam Levine. I quit my job with Angie—she was going to close the shop anyway when the cold weather set in—because I wanted to be with Peter when he came up, and we were able to manage on the money he was making. But the trouble was that we weren't really together when he got to the country. We were living on totally different rhythms.

Peter came home Friday nights saying he was

very tired, understandably. I didn't mind. I am not a very social person to start with, and after being alone a good part of the week, having Peter home was enough for me. I looked forward to long, quiet weekends with Peter, walking, talking, loving, cooking together, maybe seeing Lucy and Joe on Saturday night. I worked hard on my pottery all week so that I wouldn't have to spend much time in the shed when Peter was home. But things weren't working out that way.

What happened was that Peter became a tennis freak. He met this Cliff Wade in New York, a young actor—mainly in TV commercials—and he and his wife Diane had a weekend place not far from us. Usually Peter got a ride up with them on Friday night, and from what I could figure out, Cliff and Diane lived to play tennis. They were out on the courts all day Saturday and all day Sunday, and they hooked Peter too. They also often brought up a girl friend of Diane's, Melissa Strange, and so they had a jolly foursome. I wasn't worried about Melissa, who had fat legs and squinty eyes, but still I had to sit and watch them hit a ball back and forth calling out love this and love that.

"You could learn to play," Peter argued with me one rainy Sunday afternoon when there was no tennis. "It's a terrific game."

"But it doesn't interest me. I didn't come up here to spend my time hitting a ball over a net. I'd rather go for a walk or a bike ride. Tennis is terribly stylish, and I'm not."

"You won't even try," Peter said impatiently.

"It's not my thing. And the Wades aren't either, for that matter. They're the kind of people I wanted to get away from."

"And what's wrong with the Wades?"

"There's nothing wrong with them. I suppose they're decent people, but to me they're boring. They're ambitious and they patronize me for wanting to live the way I do. What do I have in common with Diane, who thinks the greatest thing in the world is writing copy for a cosmetic account in an ad agency? She's always making little cracks about whether I'd like her to bring me some junk for my face, when she sees plain as day that I don't use make-up."

"Maybe she's trying to be generous."

"Generous my eye. She thinks I could improve my looks."

"Well, maybe you could," Peter said.

I stared at him, dumbfounded. Then I yelled at him. "You rat. Are you telling me that I'm homely? That I'd look better if I put a lot of stuff on my face?"

"Calm down," Peter said in a soft voice. "Listen, honey, I know you're tense and nervous being pregnant, but it's no crime to say that a girl should make the most of her looks. You're beautiful, and sometimes when you do put stuff on your eyes you're gorgeous. I'm not saying you need it, but you have to admit that Diane knows how to make herself look good."

"I'm not tense and nervous because of the baby," I screamed at him. "If I am tense, it's because you're falling for a lot of hogwash. Peter, you're changing." Like a fool I burst into tears, and Peter took me in his arms to comfort me. After I calmed down, we spoke more quietly.

"Maybe I am changing some," Peter said.

But the afternoon hadn't been peaceful even before our fight. Peter was restless, first looking at the Sunday paper, then looking at the small TV he had brought up from the city a few weeks before. The day had never settled down to anything warm and cozy. Now Peter was stretched out on the sofa, the newspapers were all over the floor, and I was fixing a tuna-fish salad for him to eat before he left for the city. This week he had to be in from Monday to Friday.

"Changing how?" I asked, turning around from the kitchen counter.

"I've been thinking about this. I have no objections to living on principles. You may not agree, but I think I am, working for NET, but that doesn't exclude wanting to enjoy myself, having fun. I'd like to buy clothes; I like belonging to a tennis club. I'd love to live the way the Wades do, with an apartment in New York and a weekend place up here. I think it's great." Peter was looking at me warily.

I turned back to chopping celery. I didn't want to cry again, and I didn't want to yell. Most of all I didn't want to blow up just before Peter had to leave; I knew I couldn't bear to see him go if things weren't okay between us. I was afraid to say anything.

"You're very quiet," Peter said.

"I'm thinking."

Peter let out a deep sigh. "That sounds ominous."

Unsuccessfully I tried to laugh. "What can I say, Peter? You're telling me that you like totally different things from what I like. I like to enjoy myself too, but my idea of fun is different from yours. I'm not living on any principles, except that I prefer to steer away from a commercial world. I like to do things with my hands. I like to be as close to the earth as I can. I like to be alone with you—at least, I used to. I guess we're in different places," I added glumly.

Peter got up from the sofa and came over to me. "We don't have to be, Katie. I love you and you love me, at least you say you love me, but you're not willing to go along with me, to accept my differences from you. Remember what we said before we got married, that we weren't going to try to make each other over. But people do change, and there has to be some flexibility, some compromise."

"I'm not stopping you from doing anything you want to do. You're a free person."

"But I want you to share some of my interests with me. I think you've boxed yourself in, and you don't know how to get out. I'm sure that you'd enjoy some of the things that I enjoy if you'd only let yourself. I think you're being stubborn."

"That's unfair. I can say the same thing to you."

"But I love coming up here. I love being with you."

"You're not with me very much."

"That's what I'm talking about. I think that's your fault more than mine. You don't even attempt to do anything with me."

"Like playing tennis?"

"That's one thing."

"And when did you last go for a walk in the woods with me? Or a bike ride?"

"So I'm more gregarious than you are. I like people. I like action. I like to work with other people; you like to work alone. So we're different. That doesn't mean we have to be separate."

"Who said anything about being separate?" I asked sharply.

"I didn't mean it that way, idiot," Peter said, kissing the back of my neck and then hugging me. As always Peter's touching me momentarily stopped all talk, all panic and fears. Certainly the physical attraction we had for each other hadn't changed. In a way the differences we had made our love-making more passionate, as if we were trying to find our way back to each other, to hold on and cling to what we did have together. Sometimes I thought that the squabbling, the endless, fruitless discussions were a kind of prelude to sex—another way of building up to a climax.

When I said good-bye to Peter that night, everything was calm between us on the surface. But inside I felt confused. Was I being a bad wife? But then again that was the whole point: I did not want to think of myself as Peter's "wife," which translated meant appendage. I had to be me, myself—that was what *our* marriage was supposed to be all about. I did not want to take on Peter's personality, his likes and dislikes, and by the same token Peter should not take on mine. But if we went in different directions, how could we be together? Now I was beginning to see that we had *thought* our ideas of how to live were the same, and mine had remained the same. Peter, however, was changing, which I resented.

The craft show was the next weekend, and I concentrated on getting ready for it. As always, working in my shed was my way out, so that by Wednesday I had convinced myself that there was no problem. Peter could do his thing and I could do mine, and I was a fool to stir up trouble and to think that we couldn't go on that way. We didn't either of us believe that there had to be only one kind of marriage, and if ours was different from Lucy's and Joe's, or Cliff's and Diane's, so what? If I could only hang on to the idea that there was no one rule for the way a couple should live, I'd be okay.

Wednesday night Peter phoned to tell me that he was bringing Sam Levine and Judy Kuwolski, my old friend, up for the weekend. Sam and Judy had been going together since our wedding. "That's great," I said, "they can see the craft show." I was really glad. I loved Judy and Sam, and I felt that in asking them up Peter was trying to go back to how we used to be. Also, we wouldn't be spending another tennis weekend with the Wades.

There were a few seconds of silence on the phone. Then Peter said, "Is the craft show *this* weekend?"

"Yes, of course. I told you a dozen times." How could he forget the most important weekend in my life since we got married?

"I guess I got mixed up on the date."

"Does it make any difference?"

"Are you sure you want them to come?"

"Of course. We can all go to the show."

"We'll see."

"We'll see what? What on earth are you talking about?"

"Nothing, forget it. We'll see you Friday night. As far as I know now we'll all get a ride up with Cliff and Diane. If there's any change, I'll call you."

"Okay."

I was furious and depressed when I hung up. He hadn't even asked me if I was ready for the show, how I was doing, nothing. And he had forgotten the date. That was too much. I went out of the house and walked up the path into the woods in the moonlight. I was seething, ready to call him back and tell him to go to hell. When I stumbled on a rock, I thought, Great. Maybe I'll fall and break my neck.

Then I thought about the baby, and I started to cry. I walked with the tears streaming down my face. My poor baby was going to get born into a terrible family, a hysterical mother and a selfish father. I hugged my belly as I stumbled on. After a while I stopped crying and went home and drank some hot milk.

I tried to think constructively. So Peter had gotten mixed up on the dates, which wasn't a crime, and he had asked Judy and Sam, *our* friends, to come up. Peter was doing a marvelous job; the show he worked on was getting a lot of kudos. My parents loved him; everybody loved him. He was beautiful looking and had ideas and vitality. Peter loved me. We had a terrific sex life. What was I complaining about? I went to bed feeling lonely and a heel.

Friday was a wild day. In the morning I took my beautiful bowl, a few mugs, a pitcher, and a platter over to the craft show. The place was hectic with people setting up exhibits, hammers knocking away, and dozens of tables set up under a huge tent.

I looked around at all the people bringing in their precious objects, and I felt divinely at home. They were my kind of people, country people, old couples who never in their worst moments would allow themselves to be called "senior citizens." Women, in unstylish, baggy dresses, who worked with their hands, worked potter's wheels, made rugs, pieces of sculpture and paintings, washed clothes and dishes. Men, with ragged beards and hair, who worked with them. Young people, with bright eyes and long hair, some with babies in their arms and solemn-eyed barefoot little kids tagging alongside, depositing their wares with loving care. And I thought when he sees them on Saturday, Peter will know the difference between them and the Wades. He'll know what I mean; these are *our* kind of people.

I took a long proud look at my few pieces and my neatly typewritten card bearing my name, address, and telephone number, but I couldn't hang around. I had too much to do. I was about to leave when a young woman with long blond hair tapped my arm. "You're not going to leave these, are you?" she asked, indicating my pottery.

"I thought I was," I told her. "Shouldn't I? I've never entered a show before."

"You're very trusting. They could be stolen."

I was shocked. "Here?" I looked around at the people I had been admiring. "What should I do?"

"Bring them with you tomorrow when the show is open to the public and you're here to watch them. Probably no one exhibiting would take them, but all kinds of people wander around."

"Thanks a million for telling me." Feeling stupid, I gathered up my things and carried them back to the car. I hadn't realized I would have to stay at the show all day Saturday and Sunday, and an uneasy feeling crept over me that Peter would not exactly jump for joy at that piece of news.

I did the marketing, and then went home and cooked a big pot of spaghetti sauce for the weekend and baked a few loaves of bread. I walked down to Henry's and got some fresh-picked corn, picked vegetables and salad from our garden, and flowers for the house. I had a good time getting ready, because I was looking forward to the weekend.

The evening dragged since they couldn't possibly arrive before ten o'clock. At last I heard Cliff's car in the driveway. They all came trooping up to the door: Cliff and Diane, Melissa, Peter, Sam and Judy. Peter invited everyone in and offered them some wine. I had bought wine for the weekend, but I hadn't counted on this kind of a party. Seeing Sam and Judy, having Peter home, was wonderful, but who needed the others? I was dying to talk to Judy and Sam, but Diane got started on some long story about a mix-up she'd had in a department store. She ended up saying, "The shopgirls in New York are awful. They act as if they're doing you a favor if they sell you something. They stand around staring at you like you're dirt."

"Maybe some of their customers are," I said.

"Waiting on customers all day isn't much fun, I can tell you that. You should see the way some women drag everything out and never hang anything up."
I was sure she was one of them.

"Well, I've walked out of Saks Fifth Avenue, because no one even tried to help me."

"That was really tough on Saks," I mumbled, ignoring Peter's warning look. But Diane merely stared at me and produced one of her adorable, toothy smiles.

"I think we'd better be going, Cliff, honey. See you tomorrow morning at ten," she said to Peter.

"Make it nine thirty," Melissa said, looking at Peter as if she owned him. "We can get some practice in, Petey, before the tournament starts. If Katherine needs the car, I can pick you up." Damned if she wasn't fluttering those squinty eyes of hers.

Peter looked as if someone had just told him his zipper was open. "I'll call you in the morning," he said hurriedly.

"What is going on?" I didn't care if I made a scene, even in front of Judy and Sam. "What tournament?"

"I'll explain later," Peter said, trying to push Diane, Cliff, and Melissa out the door. But they're not easily pushed.

"The tennis tournament," Cliff said. "Didn't Peter tell you it was postponed from last weekend because of rain?"

I didn't bother to tell them that I hadn't even heard of a tennis tournament last weekend. "But the craft show is tomorrow, Peter. I've waited for it all summer."

"We'll talk about it later," Peter said tersely. He managed to get them out the door, but not before Melissa whispered something in his ear.

I was in a rage. "You'll have to excuse me, Judy and Sam, but I'm about to blow up."

"Don't mind us," Judy said good-naturedly. "But don't get your baby all riled up."

"Yes, darling," Peter said, clutching a straw, "remember our baby. It's not good for you."

"Don't you tell me what's good for me," I told him. I sat down and took a sip of wine. "Now will you please tell me what this is all about." I spoke in a calmer voice.

"It's not very complicated. The tennis tournament was postponed from last weekend, and the four of us are in the mixed doubles. We can all go to the tennis club and then to the craft show. It's nothing to get excited about." Peter's eyes on my face were anxious.

"Except that I have to be at the show all day. I

can't just leave my things there and disappear. Maybe I'll even get some orders."

Peter sat down next to me. "Then we'll come over right after the tournament. Don't get in a state, honey. It'll all work out."

"Yeah, I suppose." I was ashamed to say that I had counted on his being at the show with me. I didn't want to be there by myself all day. So I was being babyish instead of strong and independent. Yet it would have been nice if he had *wanted* to be with me.

As things turned out the next day Sam went with Peter to the tennis club and Judy came with me to the craft show. I do love Judy, but I felt awful when Peter took off. "Lots of luck, and we'll see you later," Peter said, when he kissed me good-bye.

"I hope so," I said morosely.

When we were alone in the car, Judy said, "How are things going?"

"Up and down. I'm scared. Scared of losing Peter."

"Because of Melissa?"

That scared me even more. I wasn't even thinking of her. "Should I be? Does he see her in New York?"

"I think they go to the movies once in a while."

I had a feeling Judy wasn't telling me everything, but I didn't want to hear any more. "Are you sure you want to hold on to Peter?" Judy asked.

I slowed down to let a car pass me and glanced sideways at Judy. "Of course, I'm sure. I love Peter."

"And Peter's mad about you," Judy said quickly. "But I don't think either one of you know how to be married. You've got some cockeyed notion that you can lead separate lives and still be together."

"It's not a notion—it's what we believe. And lots of people lead independent lives."

"Maybe some people can, but I don't think it's what you want. You want Peter up here leading your kind of life, and Peter wants you in New York leading his kind of life. It's that simple and that complicated."

Judy was making me feel glummer every minute. "Are you saying that you don't think we'll make it?"

Judy looked unhappy. "I'm saying that if you want to keep your marriage going, you're the one who has to work at it. The woman does—that's the way it is."

"I'll have to think about that," I said grudgingly.

The show was a complete success. Judy spelled me so that I could walk around and see the other exhibits, and I was impressed. All the beautiful objects made me feel good in one way—so many people were making such marvelous things—but they also made me feel small with my few, piddling attempts.

When I came back to Judy, she was all excited. "You got an order," she said. She had written it down: a dozen mugs for a Mrs. Connally in Pittsfield, Massachusetts. I couldn't believe it. I read that order over a dozen times. Judy had even gotten a respectable deposit.

"What did she look like? Is she some kind of a nut?"

Judy laughed. "No, she's kind of attractive, very well dressed, and she loved your things. She has a shop, which is even better."

I couldn't wait for Peter to come so I could tell him. By the time he arrived, I didn't even care that the Wades and Melissa were trailing along. I had gotten two more orders for my pitcher and the platter. It was happening, the thing I'd been dreaming of for years.

Peter was as excited as I was. Then he teased me. "The commercial world isn't so bad, is it? You like selling what you do, like anyone else."

I laughed and had to admit he was right. But I still thought that selling something beautiful that I had made was different.

"You're really good," Diane said. The surprise in

her voice was not very flattering. "Should we get some mugs, Cliff? Or maybe a darling pitcher?"

I was in a state while they debated, keeping my fingers crossed that they wouldn't buy anything. I was making a discovery: I didn't want to sell anything to someone I didn't like. I was going to hate working precious hours making mugs or pitchers for Diane, giving her my beautiful babies. Peter's enthusiasm when they finally ordered six mugs didn't make me feel any better.

Judy offered to mind shop again, and Peter and I managed to wander off *alone* to see the rest of the show. He and Melissa had come out second in the tournament, so he too was feeling pretty good. To celebrate the day, Peter bought me a beautiful pair of old garnet earrings. We had a lovely time looking at the exhibits together. If only it was always like this, I thought.

10

"I am a weekend wife," I said to Lucy on the telephone one morning in October. These days Peter was staying in the city from Monday to Friday almost every week. Lucy had no answer. There was no answer.

I felt a tremendous inertia about making any move that involved a decision. Maybe my passivity was due to the pregnancy, although physically I had been feeling fine and didn't look any different yet. I was working hard filling the pottery orders I had gotten at the show and a few more I had picked up by putting my card around in some of the local shops. The work got me through the week; I loved it, and the little bit of success I was having gave me a sense of satisfaction and an urge to do more.

The work and Lucy and Joe and David Westley. David was turning out to be a good friend. He stopped by when he could, he took me to the movies once in a while, and when I went over to Lucy and Joe's, he was often there. The thought had never occurred to me that there was anything romantic between us until one night when he brought me home from the movies. We had seen a silly picture, and we were both feeling silly.

There was a beautiful full moon, and when we got to my house, David said, "Let's go for a walk."

I thought the idea was lovely. We took my favorite path up into the woods, and David started talking about his childhood. "Van Cortland Park was the nearest I ever came to the country," he said. "It seemed really wild; some parts were and probably still are. I thought only rich people could do things like walk in the moonlight in real woods, not city woods, with a beautiful girl. When I was twelve, I never believed it could happen to me."

I laughed with him. "You don't have to be rich to do a lot of things. The best things in life are free," I sang out.

When I stumbled over a rock, David took my hand and continued to hold it. Even then I wasn't warned. We came out of the woods into a cleared field and sat down on a moss-covered rock to look at the light on the field and the mountains beyond. I was thinking of Peter, wishing that he was sitting there with me and wondering what he was doing at that moment, when suddenly David had his arms around me.

"You're an unusual girl," David said. "I'm still that little kid thinking it's a miracle that I've met someone like you."

He was trying to kiss me, and I was so surprised that I did the worst thing I could have done. I laughed. I felt awful immediately, because he looked so hurt.

"Do you think it's funny that I should be falling for you? Am I a freak or something?"

"Oh, David, no. I'm sorry. I wasn't laughing at you. I was just so surprised. . . . I mean it never occurred to me. . . ." I put out my hand and touched his arm. "I'm sorry."

David was staring glumly over the field. "It's okay. I should have known. Peter's a terrific guy, and you love him. And I'm nobody, a kid from the Bronx, a psychiatric social worker, not even an MD. A guy with a broken nose."

"Don't talk that way. You've got a wonderful face, and I love your broken nose. And I love you, David. You've been wonderful to me, and maybe I've taken advantage of your friendship." I thought of the times I'd called him when the pump wasn't working right, or I couldn't get the car started, and he had always come to help me.

"Don't be stupid. You haven't taken advantage. I'm the one who's an ass. But I guess I thought things weren't going so well with you and Peter . . . and I am crazy about you. But forget it. Come on before you get chilled. Let's go." He pulled me up from the rock.

Neither one of us talked on the way home, and he refused to come in for coffee. "I hope we can still be friends," I said, feeling silly, but I was sincere.

"Of course," David said, and he gave me a hurried good-bye kiss.

I felt terribly depressed when he left. Knowing I was still attractive to someone was nice, but then I started getting mad at Peter. He shouldn't leave me up here alone where a guy can feel free to make a pass at me. I was sitting there moping when the telephone rang, and I ran to answer it, thinking it had to be Peter.

But it was David. "I'm not calling up to apologize," he said. "I just felt like saying good-night. And I want to say one thing. If you ever do break up with Peter, put me on your list. Okay?"

"Peter and I are having a baby"—I was sure Lucy must have told him—"and we have no intention of breaking up. Thank you for the thought anyway."

If David had intended to make me feel better, the result was quite the opposite. What made him think Peter and I were going to break up? Why did everyone want us to be so conventional? Even as I pushed the irritating thought away, I knew full well that convention was the least of the problems between Peter and me.

By early November I was spending most of my days trying to keep the stove going and to stay warm. The electric heater I had in the shed was costing a fortune, and even so the clay was often too cold to work. My mother was in a state about my staying there, and Peter was trying to be understanding but looking tight-lipped and grim.

"It's not the inconveniences that I mind," I said to Lucy one day when I was visiting her. "It's being alone. If Peter were here, it would be fun and we could manage fine." I could speak this way only to Lucy, because I had sworn that I was not going to say a word to Peter, or to my parents, about his coming back to the country.

"But Peter is not here," Lucy said, "and you had better get out of there. At least look for another place up here."

Actually quiet Joe, who never said much, came the closest to understanding how I felt. "But Katherine loves that place," he said. "And I think she loves it because it *is* primitive." Then he started to laugh.

"What's so funny?" Lucy asked.

"I was just thinking of your sister. She sends her kids to a camp in the wilds of Maine where it costs her a couple of thousand dollars for each of them for eight weeks to live without any conveniences at all. She'd die if she had to live in a house like Katherine's."

We laughed with him. Joe was right. I did love that place, and I resented the fact that it was hard to manage there alone. But I was still determined to try to stick it out for the winter.

In the middle of the week before Thanksgiving Peter called up and said he was coming out on Wednesday. "That's terrific," I said. Really good news.

I built the fire up in the stove so that the house would be cosy and warm before I went to meet Peter at the bus station. He looked tired but said that he was feeling great.

As always our meetings were odd; each of us needed some time to step out of the roles we'd been in all week while apart to find our way back to each other again. By now we had developed almost a routine. First we would be quite formal with each other, making stupid conversation—how are you, did you have a good week, is there any mail (from Peter), did you talk to my parents (from me), have you been feeling all right (from Peter), have you been working hard (from me), and so forth. Then, when we got home, Peter would get out of his city clothes into old, country jeans and a sweat shirt and show the first signs of relaxation.

Then the routine could go either way. Sometimes we got close immediately, and sometimes we had a fight first. That night I was determined not to have a fight, and as soon as Peter had changed his clothes, I went over to him and put my arms around him. "This is such a lovely surprise to have you here in the middle of the week. I bought some pork chops, your favorite, to celebrate."

"That's good," Peter said, but his mind obviously was on something other than our dinner menu. He didn't push me away, but he wasn't being overaffectionate either.

"What's the matter?"

Peter sat down on the sofa and pulled me down beside him. "I came up because I want to talk to you. I have some news."

I sat up. "Good news?"

"I think so. I hope you do too." Then he grinned his Peter grin and leaned over and kissed me. "How I hate these comings and goings! Each time I have to get used to your being my wife all over again. Sure, it's good news—terrific news. I'm starting a new job the first of the year," he announced proudly.

"What, what?" My voice was excited, but just as when he told me about his present job I had a foreboding of trouble ahead.

"It's a show being packaged by a big agency for one of the major networks. A good show—I'll be an assistant producer. Cliff got me in on it, introduced me to the producer, had us to dinner together at his house. He's been a terrific friend. It's a great break." Peter's eyes were shining. "I'm really excited."

How I wished I could sincerely share his joy! "I think it's marvelous that they want you, but Peter, are you sure that's what you want? I mean, I thought you'd gone sour on the agencies and the big networks. That's why you left New York."

Peter shook his head impatiently. "You don't understand, honey. First of all this show is a good one, with great stuff in it. It's an afternoon show for women about a woman doctor, a pediatrician, and she's going to save babies' lives, poor babies in clinics. Her husband's a professional too, a lawyer, I think. They're both working, and they run into a lot of problems. It's very real."

"Like us," I said jokingly.

"Not exactly. I mean this woman works full time. She's a real pro."

"And I'm not."

"Honey, being a doctor's not quite the same as making pottery at home."

"It's not that different. But let's not get into a tangle about it." I was getting madder by the minute but controlling myself. "The idea of your working on a soap opera just seems so far removed from everything you said you wanted to do."

"Damn it, why do you put down everything that I want to do? I come home to tell you about a fantastic job, and you act as if I'm selling out. I told you it's not an ordinary show. It's a chance in a lifetime for someone like me. I can't believe my luck. I've got to build a name for myself before I can do exactly what I want."

"I don't think Ed Murrow or Walter Cronkite started off working on soap operas. If you want to be a top news reporter, you should stick to the news. I guess I don't understand."

"I can't believe you're serious. You really mean I shouldn't take this job?"

"Not if you want to be an independent newsman. This seems to me going off in the wrong direction."

Peter stared at me as if I was crazy. "Listen, remember we said we weren't going to push each other around. No manipulating. The trouble is you have no confidence in me."

"No, Peter, I'm scared. I'm scared we're losing all the things we started out with. We both wanted a special kind of life, an *unspoiled* life, nothing synthetic. . . ."

Peter took me in his arms and held me tight. As always, the minute I showed signs of weakness Peter turned warm, close, protective. "We're going to have a special kind of life," he said. "Maybe not exactly as we planned it, but an exciting, wonderful life. Someday I'm going to be big, honey, really big, and we'll go everyplace in the world and they'll roll out the red carpet for us."

No, that wasn't what we planned, I thought, but in Peter's arms I kept my mouth shut.

We had been so busy talking neither one of us had paid attention to the stove, and now the fire was out and the house cold. Cursing the stove, Peter built up the fire again. "At least, we won't have to do this much longer," he grumbled.

"Why not?"

Peter stood up and faced me. "Because you're getting out of here. You've got to come down and find an apartment for us."

I couldn't bear another battle. I was too tired

even to get indignant. "Is that an order?" I asked teasingly.

"Yes, that's an order. First, this house is unfit for the mother of my baby to live in all winter. Second, when my new job starts, I'll have to be in town all week. Third, I'm lonesome. I love you, and I didn't marry you to have you stuck up here alone. Damn it, I need you."

I was exhausted; I had no argument left in me. I was tired of battling the inevitable. As I stared out the window I saw the first snow falling. Big, white flakes cascading down. It was beautiful. I'd been waiting for the first snowfall all month. The fire was glowing and the house was warming up, all the cozier with the snow outside. I wanted to go out and run in it, to get out the sled I'd picked up in a tag sale and hadn't had time to show to Peter.

Instead I said, "I'll put on the pork chops," and went into the kitchen.

We were all sitting in my mother's kitchen, huddled around her gas stove, trying to keep warm. Our dear landlord, who was trying to get rid of his old tenants anyway, had simply neglected to order oil. I hadn't said a word about the beautiful noncomforts of city living, but Peter thought the situation as funny as I did, and every once in a while we both giggled.

On the whole, however, there hadn't been much in the way of laughs since Peter had moved me down to my parents' house while we looked for an apartment. Sleeping in my old bedroom with Peter was odd, and much as I loved my parents, living with them now as a married woman was difficult. I hated their very articulate and often expressed opinion that I was "doing the right thing." I didn't want to be doing the right thing by their standards. My brother Larry got me mad when he teased me and called me "chicken," because I didn't stick it out in the country. Still, he was the only one who said, "You were stupid to come back."

Henry had been a dear about the house, saying that he wasn't going to try to rent it over the winter, and that if we wanted it in the spring, to let him know. Peter had been packing the car when I talked to Henry, and I was glad he hadn't heard me say, "I hope we'll be back."

I alternated between feeling stupid and relieved. Stupid, because I had let myself get talked into surrendering—other people called it "compromise." Relieved, because I didn't have to battle with Peter anymore.

My days were spent tramping the streets looking for an apartment. I walked in and out of pee-smelly halls, creaky elevators, and up and down stairs, and I saw more hideous apartments than I thought existed. Anything halfway decent was much more than we could afford.

Then one Sunday, when I led Peter over to Ninth Avenue to look at a basement apartment whose one redeeming feature, in my eyes, was a five-by-six-foot yard in the back, he blew up. "Damn it, Katherine, you're looking at all the wrong things. We need an apartment, not a hole to dig in. I bet you haven't looked at one apartment in any of the high-rise complexes. You're just going out of your way to find something crummy."

"I didn't want to live in a box." I spoke meekly, because naturally he was right. I had shunned all those towering buildings clustered together that looked like gigantic prisons.

Peter, the practical one, solved the problem by finding a one-room apartment with a tiny kitchenette and bath on the fourteenth floor in a group of buildings in the West Thirties. The view was of a parking lot. The first day I went out alone I had a hard time figuring out which building was ours. I had a vision of myself sitting on a bench downstairs (don't walk on the grass; don't litter; don't talk to strangers; hang on to your pocketbook), waiting for Peter to come home.

So there I was established in New York, New York. Peter was working hard on his current job, and having lots of meetings for the new one coming up. Judy was working, and my mother was very busy at school. I discovered something that many people know already: you can be lonelier in New York than probably any other place in the world.

I didn't know what to do with myself all day. I walked the streets but seemed to have a talent for seeing nothing but freaks. "You're just imagining it," Peter said. "I see lots of attractive people."

"Maybe we travel in different neighborhoods."

One day I saw a huge man walking toward me wearing a gold brocade jacket, open Army boots, and what looked like flesh tights. When he came up close, I saw there were no tights, just his gold jacket and boots. He walked with his head in the air and seemed to be having a good time, but he gave me a turn. Some people on the street laughed, but no one paid much attention.

On pleasant days I tried sitting in the park watching the mothers and their kids. No one talked to anyone. Once a well-dressed young woman came up to me and asked if I'd give her a dollar. I did.

Peter wanted to buy me a small, electric kiln, which would be silly, because there was no room for it in our one room. Besides, when the baby came I'd be too busy.

Peter put down my depression to being pregnant, but thinking about the baby was the one thing that gave me hope. When the baby came, everything would be different. Peter and I would get close again. I was convinced.

In the meantime, we didn't seem to be any closer in New York than we had been when I was in the country. One thing I hadn't figured on was indoor tennis. I'd never even known such a thing existed, right in the heart of our great city. But Peter knew, and Melissa knew, and the Wades knew. They knew it every Sunday morning at ten o'clock, and so instead of nice, cozy, lazy Sunday mornings with pancakes and stuff, I waved good-bye to my handsome husband, whom I hardly saw all week, while he went off, racquet in hand. Sometimes I cried after he left; other times I fixed myself elaborate breakfasts, which I could not eat and hastily dumped into the garbage pail before he returned. Either way my Sundays were not hilarious.

The city was festive with Christmas decorations, and I used to love them, but now all I could think of was how pretty the snow must be on our little house and that if we had been there we could have decorated the big pine tree in the yard.

One afternoon my kid brother Larry dropped in unexpectedly to see me. "What's bugging you anyway?" I didn't know he was so sharp.

"Nothing. Why do you ask?"

"You go around like yesterday's bad joke. Trying to be funny, but no one's laughing."

His description made me laugh. "Maybe because I'm pregnant. . . ." I was getting pretty big and not at all happy with what I saw in the mirror.

"You want the kid, don't you? Peter's getting a great job, so Dad says. What's eating you?"

"Well, you see I've got a tiger in my tank and every once in a while he takes a little nibble. Not too much, just enough to make me uneasy."

Larry wasn't taken in by my attempt to be silly. "Let's make some brownies," he suggested. We did, and we had a good time. When Peter came home, the three of us ate up all the brownies, and later Peter and Larry went out and brought home some pizzas and beer. We played records, and the evening was like old times.

When Larry left and Peter and I went to bed, I decided I must be some kind of a nut. I wasn't even nineteen yet, I had everything in the world going for me, and here I was thinking of "old times." I made up my mind to turn over a new leaf.

The next morning I made a fresh start. I was going to love New York again. I cleaned up our apartment and then went for a walk up Ninth Avenue. I chatted with the fish man, stopped at the Italian fruit market and the bakery, and brought home a bunch of flowers. I had seen only one freak, a yellow-haired woman wearing a long, black lace evening dress under a moldy coat picking garbage out of a street bin. It was only eleven o'clock when I got home. I spent half an hour arranging the flowers, but there's not much you can arrange with a two-dollar bunch of heather.

But miracles do happen. The telephone rang, and Diane Wade asked if by any chance I was free to meet her for lunch. I was very free. Even excited.

I put on my one "good" maternity dress, brushed my hair, and thought, Imagine getting excited about having lunch with Diane Wade. The Japanese restaurant that she had suggested was in the West Fifties. It was a very elegant place where the customers sat on low chairs and had their food cooked in front of them by silent, smooth-skinned Japanese waiters. The food was unbelievable, and I was dying to ask for all the recipes.

The conversation did not match the food. After all, what did Diane Wade and Katherine Lundgren have in common? *Nada,* nothing. We talked about Peter and his marvelous new job with Diane getting in some good plugs for Cliff's part in the affair. We talked about the awful traffic in the city, and Diane talked about how much she'd love to have a baby but wasn't "quite ready yet." I wondered what part of her brain was earning her salary. Maybe I was just seeing the tip of the iceberg, but it left me feeling pretty chilly and sad. I saw ahead of me a long line of lunches with Diane Wades or her counterparts, whose husbands had helped give

Peter a little push along the great ladder of success. To me, ladders had always been an omen of bad luck.

I came home with a terrible headache and not at all in the mood to hear Peter say, "Diane called me and said she had a nice lunch with you. I'm glad you two are getting to be friends."

"I wouldn't exactly call it that," I said, very restrained, considering my impulse to take the fish I had bought in the market that morning and throw it at Peter.

While we were eating dinner Peter told me he had been reading some of the scripts for his new show. "The first one is terrific," he said. "It takes place in the emergency room of a hospital where the lead, this woman doctor, is in pediatrics. She's not the head—the head's a man—and they're always disagreeing except she's smarter than he is. Anyway this Puerto Rican baby who isn't breathing right is brought in, and the head guy is about to send it home, but she comes along and makes a different diagnosis. They have a great argument—a terrific scene—with the mother crying and the baby almost dying. So our girl insists on an emergency operation and saves the kid's life. It almost had me bawling when I read it."

"It sounds fantastic," I said. But I kept thinking

maybe this terrific doctor could come and save me, save me and Peter. Which was crazy, because she was only a made-up character.

Later in the evening Peter asked me if Diane had said anything about her party. I told him that she hadn't.

"I guess you two were too busy talking."

"A few words in between long silences."

Peter gave me a downgrading look. "You don't like Diane? I had thought. . . ."

"Well, you thought wrong. Nothing has happened since our intimate friendship in the country to change my mind. I can't stand her."

"Katherine, who *do* you like?"

"People. You know, real people. Whose clothes don't match, who can giggle, and who wouldn't call anyone a shopgirl. Peter, I like you. I used to anyway."

"And what do you mean by that?"

"I don't know what I mean. I mean you're different, I'm different. Something's happening to us. I don't like me either. I don't like either one of us. We're not nice to each other anymore. My head's killing me. I'm going to bed."

Peter stopped me and took me in his arms. "We don't have to be unpleasant. We're the same people. Let's just stop taking shots at each other."

"I'm agreeable."

Peter opened up our fold-up bed and got it ready for me. I curled up on my side with my back to the light where Peter was reading. But before I fell asleep I suddenly remembered and asked, "What was that about Diane's party?"

"They're giving a big party before Christmas. I thought we might walk around the Village on Saturday and find you something to wear. I'd like to get a new jacket too."

"I hate spending money on maternity clothes."

"Maybe we can find something you can use afterwards too."

"Yeah, maybe. . . ." I was aching for sleep, but the thought of a party at the Wades' became a little man scratching inside my head, who absolutely refused to let me fall asleep until *he* was ready.

12

The new dress we bought was long and blue and very full, and I looked like a fat tub in it.

"You look adorable. It's very becoming," Peter said. He put his hand on my belly, hoping to feel the baby kick. Peter's face lighted up then as if he couldn't believe there was a real baby inside.

"You're a good liar, but I'm not fooled. I look awful." We were dressing for the Wades' party, and of course my hair was being obnoxious. I finally tied it up in a knot, which wasn't half bad, at least it was better than hanging down looking like old seaweed.

Peter turned around and faced me. "You are absolutely the most beautiful pregnant woman I have ever seen. I may keep you this way indefinitely."

"I suppose you have come to this conclusion from

your intensive study of pregnant women. Have you ever been up close to one before?"

Peter laughed. "I can barely get close to you anymore. Are you ready?"

"I guess I'm as ready as I'll ever be."

Peter called for a taxi, and we went downstairs to wait for it.

The Wades lived in the East Sixties in a posh apartment house, and their apartment was what I had expected: very modern with lots of mirrors and abstract paintings, huge plants, walls painted different colors, and squishy, white rugs.

I could hardly see the furniture, because the place was jammed with people when we arrived. Terribly stylish people, a lot of them grouped around the bar, attended by a barman, and I felt sorry for two little waitresses with trays of appetizers trying to make their way through the crowd. One room had a long table piled with fabulous food.

Diane and Cliff greeted us as if they hadn't seen us in ten years and had been waiting breathlessly for our arrival. I quickly figured they must have put on this act sixty times since the party started. Poor Peter had a time maneuvering me through the crowd, with nary a familiar face in it, and finally he sat me down on a chair in a corner. When he left me to get us drinks, I felt as if I'd been deserted on a South Pacific island. But he came back, triumphant, with two glasses in hand.

"It's nice meeting you here," I offered.

"I thought we'd met before someplace," Peter said.

"Was it skiing in the Alps, or possibly Nathan's on Eighth Street?"

"Personally I thought it was in a motel on Route Seven. But I believe you wore your hair differently then."

"Oh, was that you? I was a little thinner too, I believe. Tell me, how long do we have to stay here?"

The laughter went out of Peter's eyes. "We just arrived. My new producer's over there. I'll bring him over."

"You do that."

Peter came back in a while with a Mr. Something—I didn't catch his name—who looked like ten other men in the room with fluffy hair and a mustache. They stood above me talking, and soon we were joined by none other than Melissa. She swerved down and kissed me hello, her breasts nearly falling out of her low-cut black dress, and then started talking to the men and showing off her cleavage.

I was beginning to feel suffocated when Peter bent down and whispered, "Do you mind if I circulate a bit? There are a few people I'd like to see. Business stuff."

"No, go right ahead. I've got a pretty good view from here. Like watching live TV." Peter gave me a pleading look before he disappeared into the crowd.

I was concentrating on one of the maids coming my way with some food, when an old gent came by and actually saw me.

"And what do you do," he asked, "when you're not otherwise engaged in having a baby?"

"Very little," I told him. "I sit in the park and feed the pigeons."

He laughed as though he'd just discovered the new comic of the year. "I can see you have a sense of humor."

That scintillating remark left me speechless, so we stared at each other for a while until I decided I might as well make him useful. "I'm hungry. Do you think you could perhaps get me something to eat?"

"Oh, my dear, of course. How stupid of me not to have thought of. . . ." He went off worrying like the White Rabbit, whom he actually resembled. I fully expected him to return with a plateful of carrots, but he did much better: shrimps, cheese, tiny meatballs, and some black olives. I had a feast.

I wasn't sorry when he disappeared again, and I looked around the room for Peter. He had disappeared too. Time to look for what Diane would call a powder room. The crowd parted for me as if making way for an ocean liner, and along the route I glanced into another small room and immediately wished I hadn't. It was empty except for Peter and Melissa cozily ensconced on a settee. Why Peter had wanted to circulate was all too obvious, and I suddenly felt dizzy.

I staggered into the bathroom and doused my face with cold water to calm down, but it didn't help much. What to do? Clearly the only answer was nothing, but that didn't satisfy me. I wanted to get out of that place; I wanted to go home. I was not going to play the jealous wife bit, although I was wild with hurt and jealousy, but I was *not* going back into that packed room and sit in my corner grateful for a kind word from another bore.

I did the only thing I could think of doing. I slipped on my coat and went out the door, unnoticed, and took the elevator downstairs. I found a public telephone, called the Wades' apartment, and asked for Peter. In a few minutes he was on the phone. "Peter, don't get upset. I wasn't feeling well, and I couldn't find you. Maybe I drank too much, and I needed some air. I'm taking a taxi home. . . No, you stay. . . . Honestly, please. I'd feel much worse if I spoiled your evening. I'll be all right. . . . Peter, please. It was just all the people, and the smoke. . . . I'll be fine at home. Have a good time. It's important for you. . . ."

There wasn't a thing wrong with me physically, but once in our apartment I did really feel suffocated. I paced around like someone in a cage. I kept wishing Peter would come home and dreading it. I had an awful feeling I was going to do something dramatic and stupid when I saw him. I tried to tell myself, so what, so he was sitting on a sofa with a girl, but nothing helped. My outrage came from the way he was sitting, the way he had left me alone at that dreadful party, the way we had been drifting apart, the way my belly was getting bigger.

It was now only seven o'clock, and he wouldn't be home for ages. I picked up the phone and called Lucy. She told me they had a fire going in the fireplace, it was snowing, and they had a live Christmas tree. "Why don't you and Peter come up?" she said.

I told her that Peter wasn't home, that he was at a stupid party.

"I didn't mean tonight, this minute." Lucy laughed.

"I could come. There's an eight o'clock bus," I told her.

Lucy didn't believe me. She said I was crazy. "I'm dying to see you, but I don't really think you ought to. . . ." The more she talked, the more I became convinced that I wanted to go up. "Listen," Lucy finally said, "of course, you're welcome, but just be sure it's what you want to do."

"I'm not sure of anything anymore," I said, "but I'm coming. Do you mind meeting the bus?"

I pulled off the long blue dress, put on a pair of my maternity slacks and a tunic, threw a couple of things into a bag, called for a taxi, and wrote a note to Peter:

"Hey, I talked to Lucy on the phone, smelled firewood and snow, and had to get to it, close up. Please don't worry about me. I'm okay. I'll call you and be home in a couple of days. Nothing personal—honest. Love, K."

During the ride up on the bus I had plenty of time for second thoughts. But despite my misgivings, I felt good about going away for a while.

The fresh country air smelled delicious, and there was Lucy bundled up in woolies, covered with snow, waiting for me at the bus stop. Joe was home with the kids. I was really happy to see her.

I loved being with Lucy and Joe in their simple house, but any notion I had that the visit was going to cheer me up or help solve my problems was dead wrong. I yearned to have Peter with me, and at the same time I wanted to kill him because he wasn't there and wouldn't choose to be there. Melissa didn't bother me anymore; if I were only losing him to another girl, I think I could have fought that one out—after all I still had a few tricks of my own. But what was gobbling up my Peter was not another girl; it was another world.

I was exhausted, yet wide awake, and Lucy and I stayed up till all hours talking by the fire. "So what are you going to do?" Lucy asked, after I had talked myself out, telling her the way things stood.

"What do you mean, do?" I knew very well what she meant. But I also knew that the moment there was any hint from anywhere about Peter and me splitting, I felt terribly threatened and outraged. "I'm not going to do anything. I'm going to have our baby, and I'm going to try to be a good wife to Peter. Maybe someday, when we have enough money, we can buy a little place in the country and I can have a kiln again."

Lucy look skeptical. "If that's what you want. But I think you're kidding yourself."

"I am not going to leave Peter, if that's what you're thinking," I said vehemently.

"Did I say any such thing?" Lucy looked at me innocently, then laughed. "Listen, no matter what you do, you're going to come out okay. Believe me. You're strong, Katherine."

"If I am, I can't see that it's doing me much good. Peter would probably be better off with some wide-eyed thing who thought everything he did was right."

"I doubt that he would have picked you if that's what he was looking for."

"But Peter has changed since then." We had completed the circle and were back to where we had started. It was past two o'clock in the morning, and I had no desire to go over any part of it again. Lucy kissed me good-night, and I snuggled down on the sofa, watching the fire go out, and fell asleep immediately.

Figuring that Peter had probably gotten home late from the party and would be sleeping Sunday morning, I waited until noon to call him. There was no answer. I called again at three. Still no answer. Then I thought, Okay, he knows where I am, and he can call me. But at five o'clock I tried again. This time I got him.

"Where've you been all day?" I asked cheerily.

"Out," he said coolly. "I'm the one to ask you

questions. What's the idea of running out like that? Just walking out of a party. . . ."

"I told you. I left because I was feeling woozy, and I came up here because it sounded nice. I didn't think you'd mind. You seemed pretty busy," I added.

"And what do you mean by that?"

"I meant at the party. All that circulating."

After a few seconds' silence, he said abruptly, "When are you coming home?"

"Do you miss me?"

"Don't start getting coy. Remember, that's my baby too that you're toting around everywhere."

"I'll never forget it, Peter," I said, very seriously. "When do you want me to come home?"

"That's entirely up to you."

"I miss you, Peter."

"Good. I'm glad you do." He wasn't going to give an inch.

"I'll be home tomorrow."

"Okay."

I didn't want to hang up. "What are you going to do tonight?"

"Take in a few nightclubs, of course. What do you think I'm going to do? Stay home, natch."

"I'm sorry, Peter."

"Oh, it's nothing personal. Like you said."

I felt awful when we hung up. I was tempted to

take a bus that night and go home, but Lucy wouldn't let me. It was still snowing, and she said the bus would take forever, if it was running at all, and I'd be crazy to go.

I loved Lucy and Joe and the boys, but I was restless being there. I could barely stand their coziness.

It must have been around ten o'clock when I decided to call Peter again. I knew I wouldn't sleep all night unless I talked to him once more. I let the phone ring and ring; I could hear it in our empty apartment. No answer. But he had said he was staying home, and according to the radio, it was a terrible, snowy, blowy night in New York.

"Don't panic," Lucy said. "He's probably just gone out to get something." Useless words. I did panic. I was absolutely positive he had gone to Melissa's. I tried to talk myself out of the idea, but I couldn't shake the nasty thought out of my whirling head. I tried calling again at eleven, and again at midnight. No answer. Lucy gave me hot milk and made me get into bed, but there was no sleep. I watched the dawn come up, and then finally I fell into a restless sleep.

"She's not even pretty," I said to Lucy over breakfast. "To lose Peter to that creep is just too much."

150

"You haven't lost him yet. Stop imagining things. And maybe you want to lose him. Did you ever think of that?"

"I've thought of everything, but not this. I guess I'm an idiot. I keep thinking, it's got to work, it's got to work, and if I think that hard enough, it will work."

Lucy was a dear, driving me to the bus station on skiddy roads, trying to be silly, but in my state I couldn't say a word.

When I walked into the apartment, I knew immediately that Peter had not slept there the night before. The pull-out bed was neatly folded, something he would have done on Sunday, but not this morning when he left for work. And there was no sign of any breakfast.

I slept all day, which was the easiest thing to do —no thinking, no imagining, no planning, no nothing. I was half asleep when Peter came home.

"Why didn't you call me and tell me you were back? I was worrying about your getting home. The roads must have been awful."

"The roads were okay. Peter, where were you last night?"

His eyes were startled for a second. "Why do you ask?"

"I tried calling you. Up until midnight. You had said you were staying home."

"I got restless. I went up to Cliff and Diane's. The weather was so bad I decided to stay overnight. That way I'd be nearer to work in the morning too."

I kept examining his face. "Peter, this is important. Please don't lie to me. I had an idea you'd gone up to Melissa's."

Peter didn't smile; his face showed nothing. "You get peculiar ideas."

"I notice you're not denying it."

"I don't go for this kind of cross-examination. After all, you're the one who walked out. You called and *said* you were at Lucy's. How do I know where you were? But I don't intend to push you for an answer."

Then I started giggling hysterically. "Yes, of course, there's this lover of mine who's mad for pregnant ladies. He lives in a little igloo in Central Park, and when he gets tired of his Eskimo wife, we have a rendezvous in the snow. Absolutely terrific. . . ."

Peter didn't think the routine was very funny. Suddenly the thought dawned on me that maybe I didn't want to know if he had been with Melissa or not. Because that, after all, was irrelevant.

13

Peter was trying to be sweet, and I was trying not to think about Melissa, but I don't know if we were succeeding too well. By silent agreement neither of us spoke about that awful weekend, but it hung between us like a fat mushroom cloud. Christmas came and went, and it wasn't a howling success either. We had Christmas dinner with my parents, and my mother obviously sensed that things weren't smooth between Peter and me. She kept looking at me the way she used to when she thought I was coming down with a fever.

Sure enough, after the holidays were over, my mother called me on Saturday and asked me to have lunch with her. "Dad and Larry are out," she said, "so I thought it would be a nice chance to have a real visit with you." Which, translated, meant "I want to find out what's going on between you and Peter."

Mom didn't beat around the bush. As soon as she had lunch on the table, she said, "Are you and Peter fighting a lot?"

"No," I told her honestly. Then I had to add, "I wish we were." Naturally that statement took a lot of explaining. I didn't say anything about Melissa, but I sort of brought my mother up-to-date about how Peter and I were drifting apart and how I felt about his friends and his life-style.

I let myself in for a good lecture. She told me all about the duties of a good wife, that naturally Peter wanted to get ahead, that I should help him, blah, blah, blah. . . . I do love my mother, but she can make me feel more irritated and guilty at the same time than anyone else in the world.

When she had me quite convinced I was the worst heel, my father walked in. She briefed him as to what was going on, and much to my surprise he came to my defense. "But Katherine is a person too," Dad said, sitting down at the table and picking at the cold meat and salad we had left. "She has a right to lead the kind of life that she wants. She's smart and talented and needs more than just being Peter's wife."

Mom, being very generous and tactful, didn't

point out that Dad had not been a great women's liberator in his own home. "You stand up for what you believe in," he admonished me, "and don't let anyone, not even Peter—and you know I love Peter like a son—push you around. You be yourself."

Great words. But I honestly wasn't sure who "myself" was anymore. Peter and I were having a baby, and I couldn't, and didn't, want to imagine being anyone but Peter's wife. Yet there were other me's lurking around. Katherine, the potter; Katherine in the country; Katherine thumbing her nose at ambitious, slick people; Katherine taking a stand with her husband. . . .

Peter was terribly excited about his new job. I was truly happy for him, but he was so busy that we were together less and less. When the show went on the air, I tried to watch it every day, and when Peter came home, he'd go over it in detail. Then he started worrying about the Nielsen ratings. "Are they so important?" I asked him.

"Of course. If the rating goes down, the show'll go off the air, or we'll be fired and they'll get a new production team. And it's such a terrific show, don't you think so?"

"It's soap opera," I said.

"It's not a run-of-the-mill show. It says something important, and thousands of women watch it."

I couldn't believe he was that serious about it. "Peter, I'm glad you've got the show. I really am. But you don't have to pretend it's something important. I mean, it's not so different from any other soap opera."

"Then you haven't been watching it," he said coldly. "It shows that a woman can be a good doctor, as good as a man and sometimes better. Carole Dean is a marvelous character."

He *was* serious. In order to feel that he was doing something worthwhile, he had to believe in the show. But since he was using the job only as a stepping-stone in his career, I thought that he should see the show for what it really was and not endow it with such pretentious importance. But maybe I didn't understand anything.

In the meantime, I was getting bigger and bigger and thinking a lot about my baby. I also thought about my other precious "babies," the pottery I had sold in the country, and I wondered if people had bought some for Christmas presents and if they liked the pieces. . . . I hated losing contact with the shops that had ordered my pottery. I felt cut off and shriveled in size; those sales had been a terrific lift. I also missed my nice Dr. Farnum. My mother had found me a highly recommended obstetrician, but I didn't care for him. His office and his personality were both much slicker than my country doctor's.

The Nielsen ratings apparently were okay, and Peter and his producer were riding high. The agency was talking about doing a show on prime time for the following season, and Peter was the fair-haired boy. I was married to a big success, and I was crazy not to like it.

Judy said to me one day when we were having lunch, "You may be jealous of Peter." The idea had never occurred to me, and I had to think hard about that possibility. No, I wasn't jealous of Peter's success, because it was nothing that I had ever wanted for myself. If I was jealous of anything, it was of the people that were taking Peter away from me, and away from the life we had planned together. Of course, Peter was not an innocent bystander; obviously he wanted success as much as people wanted to give it to him.

Slushy March turned into April and then May, and I began waiting every day for the baby to arrive. We had arranged that if Peter was at work and couldn't leave, I was to call my mother at home or at school. Still, I was glad that Peter was home when the time came. At six o'clock on the morning of May 9 I started having pains. We waited a little while; then Peter timed me with his stopwatch. When the pains were coming regularly, he called the doctor, who said to check into the hospital. Peter was as excited and nervous as I was, and we almost forgot my overnight bag in the excitement.

I had been doing my exercises regularly and was practising the breathing that I had learned. Fortunately, I was in labor only about three hours, and Peter was with me in the delivery room the whole time. I didn't have any anesthetic, and I always knew what was going on. The whole thing was the most exciting experience in the world.

Laura was born around five minutes after eleven. She was tiny and adorable and beautiful. Peter brought us each a darling corsage of spring flowers, and later in the afternoon my parents were there. It was a marvelously happy day. I felt great.

I was in the hospital only three days and eager to get home, but still scared about handling Laura. She was really tiny, not even six pounds. I loved her dearly and was happy to sit and look at her for hours, and I didn't mind at all waking up at night to nurse her. Having Laura to take care of kept me from being lonesome when Peter was away.

When she was a few weeks old, the doctor said I could take her out, and I walked all over the city with her in her buggy. Sometimes I sat in the park sunning myself, and I beamed like every other mother when anyone admired her. The only trouble was our one-room apartment. With the crib and Laura's paraphernalia there was no room to move.

I was so busy with Laura that for a while I stopped worrying about Peter and me. Then, when things calmed down, I noticed that he was home less and less; very often he didn't come home for dinner.

"You're quite a stranger around here," I said one night, when he came in around ten o'clock and I was feeding Laura.

Peter gave me an odd look. "There's not much room here for three of us. Besides you're so involved with the baby, I didn't think you cared."

"Aren't you involved with the baby?"

"I can't relate to her very much yet. She's beautiful and I love her, but she's usually sleeping when I see her."

"She's not sleeping now."

Peter laughed. "She's busy eating and not very interested in me. But, seriously, we've got to look for a bigger apartment. This set-up is lousy."

"Can we afford to move again so soon?"

"I think so. And I'll probably be making more money, if one of those shows for next fall comes through."

"I thought we were going to save for a place in the country." We hadn't talked about that plan for a long time.

"One thing at a time. We'll have to wait a couple of years for that step. Anyway, I meant to tell you. Cliff and Diane aren't going back to the country. They're joining a tennis club in Westchester this year instead. I told Cliff we'd probably join too. There's a swimming pool and lots of nice people."

"Oh, boy. Just what I always dreamed of, joining a tennis club in Westchester. You can't be serious." I nuzzled Laura and pushed my long hair back from falling over her. I adored holding her; having her on the outside was nicer than on the inside. It felt good to have my old figure back and be able to wear my old jeans.

"Yes, I can be serious and I am. You've been at me ever since I came back to New York and got a good job. You don't have any use for me, my friends, my work. . . . You're really an inverted snob. You look down on anyone who's successful." Peter doesn't sound off often, but when he does, he hits hard.

"Maybe you and I have different ideas of success.

I consider Joe a success, because he's a free person. He's living more or less off the land, he doesn't have any bosses, he's made himself a great house, and he has lots of time to do the things he *likes* to do. You probably consider him a failure, because he doesn't make a lot of money."

"I don't characterize people the way you do. I don't care about Joe. But what you seem to forget is that I'm doing what *I* like to do. No one's forcing me to work long hours, to care that I put on a good show. I enjoy it. I suppose I'm lucky that what I like to do also happens to pay well. I'd still like it even if I got paid less."

"I don't believe that. You said yourself you want good clothes, you like to have money and to spend it, you want a snazzy apartment, you want to join a country club. . . . You like that whole way of life."

"It's a good way. Better than an outhouse and no hot water, believe me. I suppose you'd like to wash diapers in cold water instead of using disposable ones."

"If I had the other things I wanted, I could stand it."

"Well, I don't believe you. Why don't you grow up, Katherine? You're a mother now, and it's about time you got rid of your romantic notions about living off the land. That's kid stuff. I'm going to look for an apartment, and you'll see. Once we've got a decent place, you'll enjoy it. Maybe we can find something uptown, near Central Park or on Riverside Drive." As usual, Peter cut off the argument. He decided there was enough talk, and he would solve everything with a bigger apartment.

The trouble was, Peter could still be adorable. One night he brought home two stuffed pandas, a huge one for me and a baby one for Laura. Or he would leave me a note in the morning: "Please get down on your beautiful knees and beg the Chinese laundry not to starch my shirts. I'm still a hack on Madison Avenue, not a stuffed shirt on Wall Street. I love you. P."

I couldn't stay angry with Peter, because he knew how to get what he wanted and still be lovable. That was my problem: If I could really work up a mad, and hang on to it, maybe I could do something about my own misery.

14

Not surprisingly, Peter announced a week after our unfinished discussion that we were driving up to the tennis club on Sunday with the Wades. He didn't ask me if I wanted to go; he simply said that we were going.

Sunday morning those bright eyes of his looked critically at my usual turtleneck shirt and battered slacks. "Haven't you something better to wear? We'll probably stay at the club for dinner tonight."

"All my evening gowns are in storage. Can't imagine why my maid sent them away, foolish girl. Besides, my mother taught me that if you're terribly rich you can wear anything."

My wisecracks fell flat. He didn't even smile. "Do you want to take Laura, or shall I?"

"I'll carry her if you take the basket with her diapers and stuff. I'll put in another shirt for the dinner party." I stuck an open-necked red nylon shirt in the basket, and as an afterthought I put on earrings. I did not like to be told what to wear, but I was determined to be agreeable.

We took a taxi up to the Wades (I don't know why they couldn't have picked us up in their car). After waiting around fifteen or twenty minutes for Diane to get ready—she appeared in a smashing white tennis dress—we took off.

Someone had taken a beautiful, old-fashioned mansion overlooking the Hudson River and turned it into a clubhouse. The old crystal chandeliers, the wide halls, and a curving stairway, were still there, and I felt that the ladies should be walking around the lawns and gardens in long, full skirts, their waists cinched in, twirling parasols. Instead, mini skirts, bikinis around the swimming pool, tennis dresses, long glasses of gin and tonic, diamond rings, and garish fingernails gleaming in the sunlight.

I sat under a tree by the tennis courts, wondering what I was doing there. Dopey Katherine in her old slacks and her beautiful baby. Was she going to spend her days being an accessory to a marriage? This time it wasn't squinty-eyed Melissa who made up the fourth for Peter and the Wades' game, but a handsome, dark-haired girl called Elaine. She was really a knockout, like a photographer's model, although she turned out to be a copywriter in the ad agency. Of course, I made up my mind to dislike her intensely, but she was warm and friendly, and she held Laura lovingly in her arms while I went to the bathroom. So, much to my annoyance, I couldn't work up any feeling against her. I even thought she and Peter made an attractive pair and wondered if I was losing my mind for real.

"If you want to try hitting some balls, you can use my racket and I'll hold Laura," Elaine offered.

"That's a good idea. Come on," Peter agreed enthusiastically.

I declined, politely but firmly. "No, thank you. I don't like games."

"You won't even try." Peter did not hide his annoyance with his uncooperative wife. So I watched tennis, I watched swimming, I watched drinking, and I watched Elaine trying not to flirt with Peter. I used to get a kick out of seeing girls make a play for my Peter, but now I found no amusement in that game.

When we got home, Peter innocently asked me if I'd had a good time. "I had a terrible time," I told him.

"It's your own fault. You refuse to do anything that I enjoy."

"Why does it always have to be what you enjoy? What about me?"

"I don't see you making any great suggestions."

True, I wasn't, because what I wanted couldn't be done in the framework of the life that Peter had devised for us.

But when Peter called me during the week and told me to take a taxi to meet him to look at an apartment uptown, on the East Side, I went, with Laura strapped on my back.

Peter was waiting for me downstairs, talking to a tall, red-faced doorman, who gave me a jovial greeting. "It's a good house, miss, twenty-four-hour security. You'll be safe here."

The lobby was understated, elegant. We were taken up to the third floor in a silent elevator, and the elevator man opened the door for us. The apartment was so dark that I could hardly see at first. It had a kitchenette, a living-room arrangement, a tiny bedroom and bath, and faced a courtyard, almost up against another building.

"Peter, you can't really want to live here?"

"What's wrong with it? You can fix it up to look attractive. The building's very good and so is the neighborhood. Easy for me to get to work."

I was absolutely speechless. The rent was astronomical, and the place looked like a dungeon out of a Gothic tale. "You have absolutely gone off your rocker, Peter."

"We'll discuss it later at home."

The ride home in the taxi together was silent and ominous. But as soon as our door closed behind us, we both let loose.

We really screamed at each other. Peter said that my hostility was suffocating him, that I was contemptuous of everything he did. And I told him that was absolutely true. I was contemptuous because he was turning into a Madison Avenue jerk, and it was ridiculous for us to go on living together since we had nothing in common anymore.

"If you think I'm going to give up Laura to you, you're crazy. She's my daughter as much as yours, and I'm not going to have her live in one of your crazy substandard barns."

"Are you implying that I can't take care of her? How dare you say such a thing to me. . . ." I picked up a package of diapers and threw it at him.

We sat down, exhausted. "I'm going out for a walk," Peter said wearily. "Don't wait dinner for me."

Dinner . . . who could eat? When Peter left, I burst into tears. I was terribly frightened. We could not go on this way. The thought of picking up and leaving Peter made me really afraid. If I failed at being Peter's wife, I felt there wasn't much hope for me, because he was a good, decent person. Leaving him would be so much easier if I hated him. But how could I hate Peter, who was alive, confident, physically attractive. . . . Everyone liked Peter, so obviously there must be something wrong with me.

And yet there was some knot of strength that kept me from completely giving myself up for lost. I didn't need to have everyone like me. I had had confidence once in my own point of view, in my own ideas of how I wanted to live.

I thought about the little house in the country. If I could go there for a while, alone with Laura, I could think things out. On the spur of the moment I called up Lucy.

"I've been trying to get you," she told me. "I called a few times, and I guess you were out. That woman who bought some of your pottery for her shop has been trying to track you down. She finally got to Henry, who gave her my number. She wants to give you another order."

"Are you serious?"

"Of course, I'm serious. What's the matter with you? Did you call for any reason?"

"Yes. Is our house still empty?"

When she told me that Henry hadn't rented it, I said I was coming up. "Will you tell Henry for me?"

"Terrific. You and Peter going to move back?"

I hesitated. "I'm not sure. I can't go into it on the phone. Maybe just Laura and me for a while."

"Are you okay, Katherine?"

"Yeah, I guess so. I'll call you when I'm ready to come up."

My spirits were soaring. A little order for pottery wasn't going to change my life, but I felt like someone who had just been saved from drowning.

When Peter came back from his walk, I was all excited. "The most terrific thing happened," I said the instant he came in the door. "I got an order for pottery. A reorder from the woman who bought my mugs at the craft show. I can't believe it."

"That's marvelous, but it's too bad you can't do it."

I took a deep breath. "I called Lucy and told her I want to move back to our house. She said Henry hadn't rented it."

Peter didn't say anything for several minutes. "You mean, alone?"

"You could stay here and come up weekends. The way we did before."

"But I just joined that club." The remark was so irrelevant that it made me laugh. I didn't mean to, but I did. I stopped laughing when I saw Peter's face; he was hurt and angry.

"Well, you could come up some weekends," I said lamely.

"I suppose maybe I could. When do you plan to do all this?"

"As soon as I can. Peter, it could work much better than this. . . ."

"Oh, it could work fine. If either of us wanted a half-baked marriage."

"We could try it."

Peter said nothing more, but his look told me that he didn't believe my words any more than I did.

15

It didn't take me long to get our car out of storage and pack up Laura's things and mine. Larry came over to help me load the car while Peter was at work. My mother thought I was making a terrible mistake. When I got to our house and faced living there alone with the baby, I wanted to phone Peter a dozen times a day and say, "I give up. I'm coming back."

But I didn't. Not that I had anything figured out or knew exactly what I was doing there, out in the woods without Peter. I thought about that day—it seemed a million years ago—when we sat in Pat's corner store and talked about getting married, and I couldn't bear being parted from him for a minute. What had happened to us? And then I'd start ticking off all the things that had gone wrong. Sometimes they sounded too foolish for a sane person to give up a marriage for, but other times they sounded like the most important reasons in the world.

I was sick of hearing about "lost kids" and "identity crises." My friends weren't lost, and I didn't feel lost, just confused about the choice ahead of me. I had to figure out whether to live with Peter, despite the constant struggle to keep my own identity, or whether to go it alone. I must admit I wasn't thinking of Peter's side of things too much, but when I did I decided he would have to figure out how far he wanted to go to meet my needs.

So I limped along. Peter telephoned several times, and we had terribly cool conversations, mainly about Laura. He didn't ask what I was doing or if I was coming back. My life was in limbo, like the characters in Peter's soap opera, a story that had no ending. In the meantime, Lucy and Joe, and David too, were terribly nice to me, acting as if I were recovering from a nervous breakdown or about to have one, neither of which was true. If anything, with the summer sunshine, the gardening, working at my wheel and kiln, I was getting stronger. Or so I thought.

Then, after I'd been in the country around three weeks, Peter called to say he was coming up for the weekend. Naturally he said that he wanted to see Laura, and naturally I said of course. But I was as nervous as a girl on her first date. I couldn't decide what food to buy, whether to make up the sofa for Peter, what to wear. . . . Lucy kept saying, "Just be yourself, act as you always have," but those were empty words. As far as Peter was concerned, I didn't know who I was. Was I his wife, his friend, or simply the mother of his child?

Our meeting was chaotic. The bus was late, Laura was hungry and tired, and instead of being her usual smiling, happy self, she was cranky and crying when Peter arrived. He insisted on carrying her, which made things worse, since she wasn't used to him.

"She'd better get used to me. I'm her father," Peter said impatiently.

"It takes time."

"I've got plenty of time," said Peter.

The exchange wasn't a good beginning, especially since my idea of time with a baby was longer than a weekend, but I wasn't going to get into that argument. Nothing improved when we got to the house. Suddenly I was seeing it through Peter's eyes, which put me immediately on the defensive. The house looked bare, and the few things in it were shabby. "I haven't had time to fix the place up," I said with a false gaiety. "It looks like a barn, doesn't it?"

"Barns are big," Peter said.

"I suppose I could bring up the Mexican rug from New York and the canvas chair, and when I get some pottery around, it will look better."

"You can bring up anything you want from New York," Peter said in a cool voice, and he gave me a long, hard look, which I tried to ignore.

Along with a small overnight bag, Peter had been lugging a big box from a fancy department store. He put it down on the dilapidated sofa and said, "I brought up a few things for Laura."

I was feeding her and nodded my head. "That's nice."

He was walking around, looking as if he wanted to say something but hadn't made up his mind. He went to the refrigerator and took out a can of beer —one thing I'd had sense enough to buy, thank goodness. After I'd put Laura in her crib in the bedroom, I started fussing with dinner.

"Aren't you going to open the box?" Peter asked.

"Yes, of course. I thought you might be hungry."

"I'm not."

"Well, all right. I'll open it now if you like." We were both so formal and frigid I felt like screaming.

174

I opened the box and did nearly scream. Inside were four adorable little dresses, each costing somewhere between twenty-five and forty dollars, and each needing to be hand-washed and ironed. "They're beautiful, Peter, but you may as well take them back. I'm glad you left the tags on them."

"Only to make sure the sizes were right. What's wrong with them?"

"They're silly for up here. She'll never wear them. Besides they're just not my type."

"They're not for you, they're for Laura," Peter yelled at me. "She's my daughter too, and she doesn't have to go around looking like a street kid."

I burst out laughing. "She's only a baby. How can she look like a street kid?"

"You don't even keep her clean." Peter was still yelling.

"That's a lie! She spit up a little, waiting for your stupid bus, but she's the best cared-for baby you ever knew. And I'm not going to have my kid wearing those idiotic clothes. I bet your friend Diane bought them."

"She has damned sight better taste than you have." I'd hit home. He was staring at my jeans, and then I really saw his pink shirt and his bow tie.

"I suppose she, or one of your girl friends, picked out that shirt and tie too. Maybe you ought to get an acting job in one of those commercials that provide the money you love so much. My husband, the dedicated newsman. Your idol Ed Murrow would really admire you."

Peter came across the room and slapped my face, right on my cheek. I was absolutely stunned. I screamed and yelled and called him every name I could think of, then went into the bedroom and flung myself face down on the bed and cried as I'd never cried before.

The scene was horrible. I was sobbing so hard that I was terrified I'd wake Laura up and frighten her, and I wondered if I would ever, ever in my whole life breathe again without the awful desolation that was chilling me. We weren't nice people, who came from good homes and had an education. We were screaming, obnoxious, vulgar people, who yelled and hit each other. I hated us both. I couldn't believe we could sink so low.

Then Peter came in with a contrite face and said, "I'm sorry I hit you."

"I'm sorry I said what I did," I mumbled.

He sat down on the edge of the bed with his head in his hands, looking awful. "Let's go inside," I said, getting up. "I don't want to wake up Laura."

Peter paced around the room, then stopped and looked at me. "You really like it here," he said, as if he had just made a discovery about some weird freak from a subculture.

"You don't believe it, do you?"

"I guess I haven't. I mean, I thought coming up here was a great idea, but then it got so boring. I began to think that your ideas were just a fad, a phase you were going through. And especially after you got pregnant, I was sure you'd want to come back to the real world."

"But this is a real world, much more real than yours. Your world seems the phony one to me, but let's not get into that hassle."

"No, let's not."

We sat there looking at each other, and suddenly Peter and I found we had nothing more to say. I felt sad. We, who had never stopped jabbering, never had enough time to say everything, were now like two strangers sitting side by side in a bus, wanting to strike up a conversation but knowing that only platitudes will come out.

"I suppose you're planning to stay here," Peter said.

"Yes, I am."

"There's nothing I can say to persuade you to be my wife the way I want to live. You seem to have such contempt for me."

I shook my head. "Don't say that, Peter. It's just

that—well, we're different. You're willing to do something now that you may or may not care about in order to get what you want in the future. It's a means to an end, but I don't function that way. Whatever I do has to be meaningful to me now, I suppose because I've watched my father all these years waiting for the big break. And my mother too. But the break never came, and he's wasted all those years doing stuff he hated. I don't want that, and I'm not looking for a big break. Every day is important, how I spend my time, what I do."

"And you think I'm wasting my time?"

"I think you're willing to do anything if you feel it'll get you what you want. But I believe that if you work in crummy stuff now to make money, you'll get hooked. You'll get seduced into a whole different way of life."

"Why do you assume that what I'm doing is crummy?" Peter was indignant.

"Oh, Peter, don't you see? You have to convince yourself that producing a soap opera is important, because someone's willing to pay you a lot of money to do it. But money doesn't make something important."

"And I suppose you think making a pot is important, because you made it."

"Yes, it's important to me."

"Well, I see a lot that's good in what I'm doing."

The circle was going around and around. "Let's not argue anymore. I can't stand it. But, at least, you do see that I'm not going through a phase or a fad, that I'm as serious about myself as you are about yourself. I suppose the hardest thing is for a man to believe that a woman is serious about what she wants to do."

"Katie, don't give me a lecture on this woman stuff now."

Finally I made dinner, and soon after we went to bed. There was no discussion about where Peter was to sleep. I made up the sofa for him, and then I went into the bedroom, closed the door, and got into bed with Laura's crib close beside me. Peter's sleeping in the next room was weird, and my strongest feeling was one of sadness. I felt old, as if I'd lived at least a hundred years in the past few months. And I was angry too, angry at having so much unhappiness when I was so young. I had always felt that because I was young, nothing terrible could happen to me—sad things happened only to old people. But I was finding out differently.

16

The next time I saw Peter was in New York, in my mother's house. It was in August, about a month after his visit. I drove down with Laura to bring back some household stuff my mother was giving me, and I wanted to get a few things from our apartment. Peter had been sending me some money, but I didn't want to take any more from him than I absolutely needed.

It was a beautiful Saturday afternoon. My parents and Larry were out when Peter came over. He had refused to return those baby dresses, which made me sick because Laura didn't wear them, but that day I had dressed her up in one of them for him. I honestly didn't like the way she looked—not like my baby—but Peter thought she was gorgeous.

"Let's go out for a walk," Peter said.

So there we were with Peter proudly pushing the small carriage, like an ordinary, happy family out strolling on a sunny Saturday afternoon. The picture was unreal because of the awful emptiness between us.

"How are Judy and Sam?" I asked, to make conversation.

"I haven't seen them." He must have noticed the look of surprise on my face, because he went on to explain, "I've been terribly busy on the job, and weekends I've been going up to the club."

"Yes, of course. You have a beautiful suntan." He did look marvelous, brown and healthy, and very fashionable. The girls that we passed all gave him the eye.

We walked in silence for a while. Then Peter said, "Do you want to discuss your plans?"

His question gave me a jolt. "I haven't any plans. I guess I'm just living from day to day."

"That's not the way I like to live," Peter said.

"But I have no plans beyond what I'm doing now. There's a summer craft show I want to get ready for."

"I mean plans about you and me."

"You can come up to the country on weekends as often as you want to see Laura."

"Why should I give up my weekends and have

to travel a hundred miles each way to see my own daughter? That doesn't seem fair to me."

The hostilities were on again; we were both picking up arms. "What do you suggest?"

"I think you might bring her down to spend some weekends with me."

"But Peter, she's too little. She's not completely weaned. I'm still breast feeding her."

"Maybe you had better wean her. Listen, Katie, you can't have it all your way. You left me, you chose to live out in the wilderness, but Laura is still mine as much as yours. You've got to make some accommodations."

"Don't you blackmail me with Laura. I may have left you literally now, but you left me when you moved back to New York. Don't you deny it. But whatever's happened, happened, and I don't know if there's any right or wrong. Let's try to work things out without any nastiness."

"I think we should both see lawyers and work out a legal separation or a divorce if you want."

We were standing in the bright sunshine of Washington Square Park, a block away from Nathan's, where we had decided to get married. And now, lawyers, legal separation, divorce. . . . The words felt like cold, sharp bullets, and I couldn't believe that they were meant for Peter and me.

"Do we need lawyers? I mean, can't we work things out between us?" The whole idea nauseated me.

"I doubt it." Peter was crisp and businesslike. "You're fuzzy, and I like to have everything clear-cut. I think we should at least have a legal separation, so we know where we stand . . . about money, about Laura. Otherwise, I have a feeling I'll be subject to your whims."

"My whims aren't so bad. Don't you trust me?"

Peter laughed. "That's the most idiotic question I ever heard. How do I know you won't take off for Africa with Laura?"

"But, of course, I was planning to go for the weekend. Honestly, Peter, you're really behaving like a first-class stuffed shirt."

"I'm not interested in how you think I behave. You're pretty clever drifting along, having everything your own way. Face up to the facts. We're apart, and so we may as well separate the right way."

I had a sudden thought. "Have you a girl? Do you want to marry someone?"

Peter flushed. "That's really none of your business. But I certainly don't intend to lead a celibate life."

I was sure he had a girl. And, I suppose like a million women before me, I had a terrible stab of

jealousy. Totally illogical. But my Peter. . . . I
hadn't thought about Peter marrying someone else.
I hadn't thought about marriage for myself either.

For a moment I panicked. I was out of my mind
to give up Peter. I'd never again love anyone else
the way I had loved him. He was a good, decent
human being, Laura's father. He was going to be
a tremendous success someday. We'd live in style,
Laura would go to the best schools and wear the
finest clothes, we'd walk in the park every Saturday, we'd have dinner parties Saturday nights. . . .
I wouldn't have to go to a lawyer and figure
out money and visitations—hideous word—and go
through a lot of claptrap to get unmarried from
Peter. I stood there in Washington Square Park and
felt as if I were shooting dice with my life. I could
still turn back or go ahead. . . .

"What's the matter with you? You look green.
Don't get sick here." Peter was looking at me with
efficient, unfriendly eyes. A skinny girl with long
hair, in jeans and a turtlenecked shirt, not at all
the kind of girl he wanted for his wife. Slowly my
thumping heart subsided back to its normal beat.

"Don't worry, I'm not going to get sick. I won't
disgrace you."

Peter laughed, but what I'd said wasn't so funny.

There was no turning back. Peter had faced the

184

facts better than I, which was not surprising, since I am not a very good fact facer.

Before Peter left me that afternoon he insisted that he have Laura all day Sunday. He was going to take her up to his club. I tried all kinds of excuses —she might not take the bottle, she wasn't used to him yet, there was no one to watch her while he was playing tennis—but he had an answer for each one of them. And in all fairness, I couldn't deny his right to have Laura to himself for a day.

"You see what I mean," Peter said. "We've got to have everything understood and arranged between us. I don't want this kind of hassle every time I want to see Laura."

Sunday was another gorgeous day, and I wanted more than anything to get in the car and drive right back to the country with Laura. Life was crowding in too fast; I couldn't think in New York and I needed to get things straight in my head. But bright and early Peter came around to pick up the baby. I gave him a bag, with bottles and diapers and jars of baby food, and a list of instructions. When he went out the door with Laura in his arms, I thought I'd die.

Larry scolded me. "Listen, she's his kid too, isn't she? You act like he's kidnapping her."

"Please shut up," I told him.

Before Peter had left, I told him that I was going to pick up some things from our apartment that afternoon. He had hesitated for a few minutes before he said, "Of course, take whatever you want." Then he added, "When you leave would you just put your key on the kitchen counter. The door will lock automatically." I must have looked questioning. "You don't need the key anymore, do you?" he asked.

"No, I guess not," I said.

Suddenly I realized that it wasn't our apartment anymore; it was Peter's. We were now separate persons whose only connection was Laura. I kept thinking, "He's so cool. What is *he* feeling? Does he cry in the night? Is he glad to be rid of me? He was acting the perfect gentleman, generous about money, letting me take whatever I wanted, but what was he *feeling*? Peter would never let me know. I would never know again how Peter felt about anything.

My mother and father both tried to be terribly nice to me, but I couldn't bear their sympathy. After all, Peter wasn't divorcing me. I had to keep reminding myself that I did not want to live with him. Still, I spent a long, dreary day, waiting for Laura to come home.

In the afternoon I went over to our apartment. My mother wanted to come with me, but I preferred to go alone. The place was very neat and orderly, as I knew it would be, and I collected a few things in a hurry. I felt like a trespasser and wanted to get out fast. I was grabbing my clothes out of the closet, when I realized I had a long, pale yellow robe in my arms that wasn't mine. I dropped it like a hot coal. Then I dropped everything and sat down on the bed, but I quickly got up and sat on a chair. So I was right. Peter did have a girl or at least someone who had been with him in the apartment. A girl with a pale yellow robe.

Of course. Why not? Still, this proof of her existence was a period at the end of a long story, the final curtain coming down on a play in many acts. Everything between Peter and me had been moving to this conclusion for many months. Whatever came now, whatever the lawyers agreed upon was inconsequential . . . our marriage was over.

I don't know how long I sat there, minutes, hours. . . . And then a strange thing happened. I felt a great relief, as if someone had tapped me on the shoulder and said, "Hey, kid, you're free. You don't owe anybody anything."

Then I realized I'd been feeling guilty about Peter, about Laura, about needing to go my own way. But that yellow robe freed me. There was a great big world out there, and I was going to hack it on my own, with my pottery, with my little shacky house, with my lovely daughter, with my few beautiful friends.

I looked around the apartment and decided that I didn't want anything except a few personal things. I put the key on the kitchen counter, blew it a good-bye kiss, and went out with my clothes, my books, a couple of pictures, and records.

Back at my mother's I waited for Peter to bring Laura home. The hardest part was going to be sharing Laura with Peter, with Peter and some unknown girl he would undoubtedly eventually marry. But as Peter had so pointedly said, I couldn't have everything my own way and I had better accept the compromises gracefully. Laura was not going to suffer or be a battleground between Peter and me, and I made up my mind to learn right at the beginning not to be jittery every time she went to Peter.

I sat and talked with my parents, and when Peter did come in with Laura I think I put on a pretty good show of the relaxed mother. He was all apologies for being late, which he was, and was quite taken aback that I wasn't furious.

The next morning, when I was saying good-bye to my parents, my mother said, "Are you going to be all right?"

188

"I'm going to be fine," I told her. And they weren't meaningless words. I meant them.

"Aren't you afraid to be alone?"

"No, I've been alone before. And I have Laura. Listen, Mom," I said, answering the worried look on her face, "I don't expect things to be easy, but what I'm most afraid of is leading a phony life. I've got to live my own way. Don't worry about me."

"She'll be okay," my father said, and I kissed them both gratefully. They might be anxious, but I think they really understood.

My dad helped me load the car, and with Laura safely belted into her car seat I drove back to my own house, ready to face what lay ahead.

Hila Colman was born and grew up in New York City, where she went to Calhoun School. After graduation, she attended Radcliffe College. Before she started writing for herself, she wrote publicity material and ran a book club. Her first story was sold to the *Saturday Evening Post,* and since then her stories and articles have appeared in many periodicals. Some have been dramatized for television. In 1957 she turned to writing books for teen-age girls. One of them, *The Girl from Puerto Rico,* was given a special citation by the Child Study Association of America.

Mrs. Colman and her husband live in Bridgewater, Connecticut. They have two sons, both of whom are married.